James Hadley Chase and The Murder Room

>>> This title is part of The Murder Room, our series dedicated to making available out-of-print or hard-to-find titles by classic crime writers.

Crime fiction has always held up a mirror to society. The Victorians were fascinated by sensational murder and the emerging science of detection; now we are obsessed with the forensic detail of violent death. And no other genre has so captivated and enthralled readers.

Vast troves of classic crime writing have for a long time been unavailable to all but the most dedicated frequenters of second-hand bookshops. The advent of digital publishing means that we are now able to bring you the backlists of a huge range of titles by classic and contemporary crime writers, some of which have been out of print for decades.

From the genteel amateur private eyes of the Golden Age and the femmes fatales of pulp fiction, to the morally ambiguous hard-boiled detectives of mid twentieth-century America and their descendants who walk our twenty-first century streets, The Murder Room has it all. **>>>**

The Murder Room
Where Criminal Minds Meet

themurderroom.com

James Hadley Chase (1906–1985)

Born René Brabazon Raymond in London, the son of a British colonel in the Indian Army, James Hadley Chase was educated at King's School in Rochester, Kent, and left home at the age of 18. He initially worked in book sales until, inspired by the rise of gangster culture during the Depression and by reading James M. Cain's *The Postman Always Rings Twice*, he wrote his first novel, *No Orchids for Miss Blandish*. Despite the American setting of many of his novels, Chase (like Peter Cheyney, another hugely successful British noir writer) never lived there, writing with the aid of maps and a slang dictionary. He had phenomenal success with the novel, which continued unabated throughout his entire career, spanning 45 years and nearly 90 novels. His work was published in dozens of languages and over thirty titles were adapted for film. He served in the RAF during World War II, where he also edited the RAF Journal. In 1956 he moved to France with his wife and son; they later moved to Switzerland, where Chase lived until his death in 1985.

By James Hadley Chase
(published in the Murder Room)

No Orchids for Miss Blandish (1939)
Eve (1945)
More Deadly Than the Male (1946)
Mission to Venice (1954)
Mission to Siena (1955)
Not Safe to Be Free (1958)
Shock Treatment (1959)
Come Easy – Go Easy (1960)
What's Better Than Money? (1960)
Just Another Sucker (1961)
I Would Rather Stay Poor (1962)
A Coffin from Hong Kong (1962)
Tell it to the Birds (1963)
One Bright Summer Morning (1963)
The Soft Centre (1964)
You Have Yourself a Deal (1966)
Have This One on Me (1967)
Well Now, My Pretty (1967)
Believed Violent (1968)
An Ear to the Ground (1968)
The Whiff of Money (1969)
The Vulture Is a Patient Bird (1969)
Like a Hole in the Head (1970)
An Ace Up My Sleeve (1971)
Want to Stay Alive? (1971)
Just a Matter of Time (1972)
You're Dead Without Money (1972)
Have a Change of Scene (1973)
Knock, Knock! Who's There? (1973)
Goldfish Have No Hiding Place (1974)
So What Happens to Me? (1974)
The Joker in the Pack (1975)
Believe This, You'll Believe Anything (1975)
Do Me a Favour – Drop Dead (1976)
I Hold the Four Aces (1977)
My Laugh Comes Last (1977)
Consider Yourself Dead (1978)
You Must Be Kidding (1979)
A Can of Worms (1979)
Try This One for Size (1980)
You Can Say That Again (1980)
Hand Me a Fig-Leaf (1981)
Have a Nice Night (1982)
We'll Share a Double Funeral (1982)
Not My Thing (1983)
Hit Them Where It Hurts (1984)

Knock, Knock! Who's There?

James Hadley Chase

An Orion book

Copyright © Hervey Raymond 1973

The right of James Hadley Chase to be identified as the author of this work has been
asserted in accordance with the Copyright, Designs and Patents Act 1988.

This edition published by
The Orion Publishing Group Ltd
Orion House
5 Upper St Martin's Lane
London WC2H 9EA

An Hachette UK company
A CIP catalogue record for this book is available from the British Library

ISBN 978 1 4719 0382 3

www.orionbooks.co.uk

1

The drizzling rain fell on Sammy the Black's sweating face as he shuffled along carrying the bag of money. He was a tall, gangling negro of around thirty years of age. With the muscular shoulders of a boxer and huge hands and feet, few would guess he had the spirit of a mouse. His large black eyes rolled fearfully as he walked, aware that he was carrying some sixty thousand dollars in the shabby hold-all and what was worse that everyone in the district knew it.

Every Friday, at exactly the same time, he did this long walk which took four hours. During those hours, he collected money from bars, newsstands and from the Numbers men. During this stop-start walk, Sammy sweated with fear, expecting at any moment some nut would shoot him down and grab the money.

For five hundred and twenty Fridays, he had done this walk and even after so many Fridays when nothing had happened, he couldn't shake the fear out of his system. He kept telling himself that if it wasn't this Friday, it could be the next.

Sammy couldn't believe, even after ten years, in the power of his boss, Joe Massino. He couldn't believe that any one man could have this sprawling town of close on half a million inhabitants in such a relentless grip that no one – not even a nutter – would dare attempt to steal the bag of money that Sammy was carrying.

1

Sammy had told himself often enough that he was crazy to be so scared since Johnny Bianda was always with him and Johnny was considered the best gunman of Massino's mob.

"If anything happens, Sammy," Johnny had said, time and again, "fall on the bag and leave the rest to me."

These should be comforting words, but they didn't comfort Sammy. The fact that even Johnny thought something could happen turned Sammy sick to his stomach.

All the same, he told himself, it was a lot better than nothing to have Johnny's protection. He and Johnny had been Massino's collectors now for the past ten years. Sammy, at the age of twenty, had taken the job because the money was good and his nerves were in much better shape than now. Also, in spite of his fear, he was proud to have been picked as Massino's collector for that meant the boss trusted him. Well, maybe not quite trusted him for Johnny always went along and there was a foolproof system against a fiddle. Sammy was given a sealed envelope containing the money and Johnny a sealed envelope containing a signed chit stating the amount of the money. It was only when they got back to Massino's office and stood around while the money was being counted that they learned the amount they had collected and the amounts, during the ten years they had been collectors, increased every year until the take on the previous Friday had been the alarming (to Sammy) sum of sixty-three thousand dollars!

Sure, in spite of Massino's ruthless reputation and Johnny's ability to shoot fast, some nutter would be tempted to snatch the money, Sammy thought as he trudged along. He looked uneasily around him. The busy, shabby street teemed with people who made room for him, grinning at him and calling out to him.

A big, black buck, nearly as big as Sammy bawled from the steps of a tenement, "Don't lose it, Sammy ol' boy, ol' boy. That little ol' bag's got my winnings!"

The crowd laughed and Sammy, sweating more heavily, lengthened his stride. They had one more call to make before they could get into Johnny's beat-up Ford and Sammy could relax.

Watched by the crowd, they walked into Solly Jacob's betting office.

Solly, vast, with a tremendous paunch and a face that looked as if it had been fashioned out of dough, had the envelopes ready.

"Not bad this week," he said to Sammy, "but tell Mr Joe, next week is going to be a bonanza. February 29th! Every sucker in town will be trying his luck. Tell Mr Joe you'll need a truck to bring the money in. Don't kid yourself you'll be able to carry it."

Sammy cringed as he put the envelope in the bag.

"And, Johnny," Solly said, handing Johnny his envelope, "maybe it would be an idea to get more protection for Sammy next week. Have a word with Mr Joe."

Johnny grunted. He was a man of few words. He turned to the door and went out into the street, followed by Sammy.

They had only a few yards to walk to where Johnny had parked his car and with relief Sammy got into the passenger's seat. The handcuff around his thick wrist was chaffing his skin. That was another thing that scared him: to be handcuffed to the bag! He had once read of some bank clerk who had had his hand chopped off with an axe by some nutter, trying to get the bag from him. To be without a hand!

3

Johnny sank into the driving seat and searched for the ignition key. Sammy looked uneasily at him. He had an idea that Johnny had something preying on his mind. For the past few weeks, Johnny had been more silent than he had ever been. Yes, Sammy was sure something was preying on his mind and this worried him because he was fond of this short, thickset man with his thick black hair, shot with grey, his deep-set brown eyes and his firm, hard mouth. Sammy knew Johnny was as tough as teak and he carried a punch like a sledgehammer blow. Sammy had never forgotten how Johnny had once handled a punk who had tried to pick a quarrel. He and Johnny were enjoying a beer in a down-town bar when this punk, twice Johnny's size, came up and said in a voice like a fall of gravel that he didn't drink in the same bar as a nigger.

Johnny had said quietly, "Then drink somewhere else."

That was something Sammy always admired about Johnny: he always spoke quietly: he never shouted.

The punk had turned on Sammy who was sweating with fright, but Johnny had stepped between them so the punk had hit him. To Sammy, it seemed a hell of a punch, but Johnny didn't even grunt. He swayed a little, then the punk took a bang on the jaw that broke it and flattened him. Sammy hadn't seen the punch: it had been too fast, but he had seen the effect.

Yes, Johnny was as tough as teak, but he was fine with Sammy. He didn't talk a lot. In fact, Sammy, after going around with him for ten years, knew little or nothing about him except that he had been Massino's gunman for some twenty years, was maybe forty-two or three years of age, unmarried, no relations, lived in a two-room apartment and Massino thought a lot of him.

Whenever Sammy got worried or had woman trouble or his young brother was playing up or something he would consult Johnny, and Johnny, speaking in his quiet voice, always managed to make Sammy feel good even if he didn't solve his problem.

When they began the collection together, Johnny had been more talkative. He had said something that Sammy had never forgotten.

"Listen, Sammy," Johnny had said. "You'll make good money from this racket, but don't let it kid you. You put by ten per cent of what you earn every week. Understand? Out of every ten dollars you earn, put one dollar aside and don't touch it. In a few years you'll have enough to be independent and you can get out of this racket, for as sure as God made little apples, sooner or later, you'll want to get out."

Sammy had followed this advice. It made sense to him. He bought a steel box and every week when he got paid he put ten per cent of his earnings in the box which he kept under his bed. Of course there had been times when he had been forced to milk the box. There was that business with his brother who had to have five hundred dollars or go to jail. Then there was that business with Cloe who had to have an expensive abortion, but over the years the ten per cent mounted up and the last time Sammy checked the amount he was astonished to find he was worth three thousand dollars.

The box which wasn't large was getting too full of ten dollar bills for comfort and Sammy began to worry whether to buy another box. There was something about Johnny these days that made him hesitate to ask his advice. He was sure Johnny had something on his mind and he didn't want to be a nuisance. He thought maybe he would wait a little longer before consulting him. Maybe he would get whatever it was off his mind and then, he would be in the mood to advise him.

They drove in silence to Massino's office: a large room with a big desk, a few chairs and a filing cabinet. Massino believed in austerity when he was downtown, although he had a Rolls, a sixteen-bedroom house uptown, a yacht and a ten-bedroom house in Miami.

He was at his desk when Johnny and Sammy came in. Leaning against the wall was Toni Capello, one of Massino's bodyguards: a thin, dark man with snake's eyes and nearly as fast as Johnny with a gun. Sitting on a hard backed chair, picking his teeth with a splinter of wood was Ernie Lassini, another of Massino's bodyguards: a fat, hulking man with a razor scar down the left side of his face: another good man with a gun.

Sammy shambled up to the desk and put the bag in front of Massino who leaned back in his chair and grinned at the bag.

At the age of fifty-five, Joe Massino was massively built. Medium height, he had barn-door shoulders, no neck, a heavy fat face with a flattened nose, a straggly moustache and bleak grey eyes that scared men, but intrigued women. Massino was a great womanizer. Although fat, he was still tough and there had been times when he had personally disciplined one of his mob and that man hadn't been fit for active service for two or even three months.

"No problems, Sammy?" Massino asked and his small grey eyes shifted to Johnny who shook his head. "Okay ... get Andy."

But Andy Lucas, Massino's accountant, had already come into the office.

Andy was sixty-five years of age: a tiny, bird-like man with a computer for a brain. Fifteen years ago he had served a stretch for fraud and when he had come out, Massino, realizing Andy's brilliance, had hired him to control his financial kingdom. As with most things Massino did, this was a wise choice. There was no one in the State as smart as Andy when it came to a tax form, an investment or an idea to make money.

Andy unlocked the handcuff from Sammy's sweating wrist, then pulling up a chair by Massino, he began to check the contents of the bag while Massino watched as he chewed a dead cigar.

Both Sammy and Johnny moved away and waited. The count came to sixty-five thousand dollars.

Andy put the money back in the bag, then nodding to Massino, he carried the bag into his office and put it in the big, old-fashioned safe.

"Okay, you two," Massino said, looking at Johnny and Sammy, "take time off. I don't need you until next Friday. You know what next Friday is?" His hard little eyes rested on Johnny.

"The 29th."

Massino nodded.

"That's it; the freak day: Leap year's day. It's my bet the take will be around $150,000."

"Solly said the same."

"Yeah." Massino dropped the dead cigar into the trash basket. "So ... Ernie and Toni will go with you. You'll collect in the car. Never mind the traffic. I'll have a word with the Commissioner. Next Friday, the cops will look the other way if you have to double park. $150,000 is a hell of a lot of money and maybe some hop-head just might try,"

He eyed Sammy. "Take it easy, boy, you'll be protected. Don't sweat so."

Sammy forced a sick grin.

"I'm not worried, boss," he lied. "You tell me what to do and I'll do it."

Out in the drizzle, Johnny said, "Come on, Sammy, let's have a beer."

This was the usual ritual after the collection and Sammy walked along beside the short, thickset man, gradually relaxing until they came to Freddy's bar. They went into the warm darkness, climbed on stools and ordered beer.

They drank in silence, then Sammy ordered more beer.

"Mr Johnny ..." He paused and looked uneasily at the hard, expressionless face. "Excuse me, but have you got worries? You're sort of quiet these days. If there's anything I can do ..." He began to sweat, scared he had talked out of turn.

Johnny looked at him and smiled. Johnny didn't often smile, but when he did it sent a glow of happiness through Sammy.

"No ... there's nothing." He lifted his heavy shoulders. "Maybe I'm getting old. Anyway, thanks, Sammy." He took a packet of cigarettes, rolled one towards Sammy and lit up. "This is a hell of a life, isn't it? No future in it for us." He let smoke drift down his nostrils, then asked, "How do you feel about it, Sammy?"

Sammy shifted on his stool.

"The money's good, Mr Johnny. I get scared, but the money's good. What else could I do?"

Johnny regarded him, then nodded.

"That's right ... what else can you do?" A pause, then he went on, "Have you been saving?"

Sammy smiled happily.

"Just like you told me, Mr Johnny. One dollar in ten. That's what you said and now I've got three thousand bucks in a box under my bed." He lost his smile as he paused. "I don't know what to do with it."

Johnny sighed.

"You keep all that money under your bed?"

"What else can I do with it?"

"Put it in a bank, you goon."

"I don't like banks, Mr Johnny," Sammy said earnestly. "They're for white men. It's best under my bed. I guess I'll have to buy another box."

Although Sammy looked hopefully at Johnny wanting him to solve this problem, Johnny shrugged and finished his beer. He couldn't be bothered with Sammy's stupid problems. He had too many problems of his own.

"Please yourself." He slid off the stool. "Well, see you next Friday, Sammy."

"Do you think there'll be trouble?" Sammy asked fearfully as he followed Johnny out into the drizzle.

Johnny saw the naked fear in Sammy's big, black eyes. He smiled.

"No trouble. Not with me, Ernie and Toni with you. Take it easy, Sammy ... nothing will happen."

Sammy watched him drive away, then he set off along the street towards his pad. Friday was a long way off, he told himself. $150,000! the Boss had said. Was there that much money in the world? *Nothing would happen.* He'd believe that when Friday was over.

* * *

Johnny Bianda unlocked the door of his two-room apartment. He moved into the big living-room and paused

9

to look around. He had lived in this apartment now for the past eight years. It wasn't much, but that didn't worry Johnny. At least it was comfortable, although shabby. There were two battered lounging chairs, a settee, a TV set, a table, four upright chairs and a faded carpet. Through the door opposite was a tiny bedroom that just took a double bed and a night table with a built-in closet. There was a shower and a loo off the bedroom.

He took off his jacket, loosened his tie and parked his .38 automatic, then pulling up a chair to the window, he sat down.

The noise from the street drifted up to him. Noise never bothered him. He lit a cigarette and stared through the dirty window pane at the apartment block without seeing it.

Sammy had been right in guessing he had something on his mind. This something had been on his mind now for the past eighteen months. It had begun to nag him on his fortieth birthday. After celebrating with his girl friend, Melanie Carelli, and when she had fallen asleep, he had lain in the darkness and had thought about his past and had tried to imagine what his future was going to be. Forty years old! The half-way mark ... always provided he didn't have an accident, got lung cancer or stopped a bullet. Forty years old! His life half over!

He had thought of the years that had moved behind him. First, he thought of his mother who hadn't been able to read or write and who had worked herself to an early death to keep a roof over his head while his father who had been able to read but not write had slaved in a fruit-canning factory: two decent God-fearing Italian immigrants who had loved him and had hoped for great things from him.

Just before she had died, his mother had given him her only possession: a silver St Christopher medal on a silver chain that had been in her family for over a century.

"There's nothing more I can do for you now, Johnny," she had said. "Take this: wear it always: as long as you wear it nothing really bad can happen to you. Remember that. I've worn it all my life and nothing really bad has happened to me. It's been hard, but not really bad."

He had been superstitious enough to have worn the medal and even now as he sat by the window, he put his fingers inside his shirt to touch the medal.

Lying by the side of the gently breathing Melanie, he had thought of the years after his mother's death. He hadn't settled to anything. He had got tired of his father's constant nagging and had left home. Although only seventeen, he had got a job as a bartender in a dive in Jacksonville. There he associated with the wide boys, the little crooks and the petty con men. He had hooked up with Ferdie Ciano, a small time heist man. Together, they had pulled a number of jobs, mostly gas stations until the police caught up with them. Johnny did a two-year stretch and that decided his fate. He came out of prison, educated in crime and sure that next time he wouldn't be caught. For a couple of years he worked solo as a stick-up man. The money hadn't amounted to anything but he was always hoping for something big. Then he ran into Ciano again who was now working for Joe Massino, an up and coming gang leader. Ciano took him along and Massino looked him over. He thought Johnny was made of the right material. He had been looking for a young, reliable man, good with a gun, to act as his bodyguard. Johnny knew little or nothing about guns. As a stick-up man he had used a toy pistol. This didn't bother Massino. He had Johnny trained. After three months, Johnny proved himself to be a top-class shot and during the years of Massino's rise to power, Johnny had killed three times, saving Massino's life each time from certain death. Now, he had been with Massino for the past twenty years. There were no more killings. Massino was firmly in the saddle. He not only controlled the Unions in this big town, but also the Numbers racket and there was no one powerful enough to challenge him. Johnny was no longer his bodyguard. He had been assigned to take care of Sammy when Sammy collected the money for the Numbers pay-off. Massino believed in having young men to protect him. Anyone over thirty-five was too old, too slow for protection.

Lying on the bed beside Melanie, Johnny had thought about all this and then turned his mind to his future. Forty years of age! If he didn't do something soon, it would be too late. In another two or three years, Massino would begin to think he was getting too old to guard Sammy. Then what? No golden handshake for Johnny ... that was for sure. He would be offered a job, probably counting Union votes, running errands or some such god-awful thing. It would be the kiss-off. He had never been able to save money. His mouth had twisted into a wry grin as he remembered the advice he had given Sammy. Somehow his money had slipped through his fingers: women, his fatal weakness for listening to any hard luck story and betting on horses that never showed. Money came and went, so he knew when Massino gave him the kiss-off he wouldn't have enough to live on the way he wanted to live nor to do what he had always longed to do.

Ever since he could remember, he had dreamed of owning a boat. When he was a kid he had spent all his spare time down at the harbour where the rich had their yachts and the fishermen their boats. The sea had pulled and still pulled him like a magnet. When he should have been at school, he was messing around in boats. He didn't care how hard he worked or what he was paid so long as he was allowed on board. He scrubbed decks, polished brass and spliced ropes for nickels. He still thought back on that time when he was a kid: the best time of his life!

Lying in the dark, he again felt the compulsive urge to return to the sea, but not as a kid working for nickels and sweating his heart out just to feel the lift and fall of a deck under his feet. He wanted to return with his own boat: a sleek thirty-footer and he would charter her for fishing: going along as Captain with one crew – someone like Sammy: even Sammy.

The boat of his dreams would cost money: then there was the heavy fishing tackle and the first running expenses. He reckoned he would need at least $60,000.

He told himself he was crazy in the head to be thinking like that, but that didn't stop him thinking nor dreaming. Like an aching tooth, the dream of owning his own boat, feeling the surge of the sea nagged him for as long as he could remember and was nagging him now as he sat at the window.

A dream that could come true if he could lay his hands on a large sum of money.

Some six months ago an idea had dropped into his mind which he had immediately shied away from ... shutting it away like a man who feels a sudden stabbing pain shuts away the thought of cancer. But the idea kept coming back. It even haunted his dreams until finally, he told himself an idea was just an idea: it could be looked at, couldn't it? There was no harm in looking at it, was there?

And when he began to look at it, he realized for the first time what it meant to be a loner. It would have been so much better, so much more reassuring if he had someone to discuss the idea with, but there was no one: no one he could trust. What was the use of talking about a thing like this with his only real solid friend: Sammy the Black? What use would Melanie be if he told her what was going on in his mind? She would hate the idea of the sea and a boat. She would think he had gone crazy. Even if his mother had been alive, he couldn't have talked to her about it. She would have been horrified. His father had been too dumb, too much of a slave, to discuss with him any goddamn thing.

So he had looked at this idea when he was alone as he was now beginning to look at it again while sitting at the window.

Simply stated, the idea was for him to steal the Numbers collection, but to justify the high risk, he had, he told himself, to wait patiently until the big take came along as he knew it must from his past experience as a collector.

And now here it was! February 29th! Something like $150,000! The big take!

If I'm going to do it, if I'm ever going to own that boat, Johnny thought, Friday 29th is D-day! With that kind of money, I can buy a good boat, have money over so if the fishing charter idea flops, it won't matter. With that kind of money and living carefully, I can last out until I die and still have the boat, the sea and nothing to worry about. I swear I'll kiss the horses good-bye. I might even kiss the chicks goodbye and I'll shut my ears to any future hard luck story!

Well, okay, he said to himself, as he settled his bulk more comfortably in the old lounging chair, so on Friday night of the 29th, you go ahead and take this money from Massino. You've thought about it long enough. You have made plans.

You have even gone so far as to take an impression of the key of Andy's safe. You have gone even further than that: you have made a duplicate key from the impression that you know will open the safe. That was where those two years in jail had paid off: you learned things like taking key impressions and making keys from the impressions.

He paused here to recall just how he had got the impression and tiny beads broke out of his forehead when he remembered the risk he had run.

The safe was a big hunk of old-fashioned metal that stood in Andy's tiny office, facing the door. The safe had belonged to Massino's grandfather.

More than once, Johnny had heard Andy complain about the safe to Massino.

"You want something modern," Andy had said. "A kid could bust into this goddamn thing. Why not let me get rid of it and fix you with something modern?"

Johnny well remembered Massino's reply.

"That safe belonged to my grandfather. What was good enough for him is good enough for me. I'll tell you something: that safe is a symbol of my power. There's no one in this town who dare touch it except you and me. You put the take in there every Friday and everyone in this town knows the take will be there on Saturday morning for the pay out. Why? Because they know no one would have the guts to touch anything that belongs to me. That safe is as safe as my power ... and let me tell you, my power is very safe!"

But Andy had tried again.

"I know all that, Mr Joe," he had said while Johnny had listened, "but there might be some out-of-town nutter who couldn't resist trying. So why take a chance?"

Massino had stared at Andy, his eyes like little pools of ice.

"If anyone busts into that safe, I go after him," he said. "He wouldn't get far. Anyone who takes anything from me had better talk to a grave-digger ... but they won't. There's no one dumb enough to try to take anything from me."

But Massino hedged his bets. He had done that most of his life and it had paid off. When the Numbers money was locked in the safe on Friday, he left Benno Bianco locked with the safe in Andy's office. Not that Benno was anything special. He had once been an up and coming welter-weight, but he hadn't got very far. He was pretty good with a gun and he looked tough: a lot tougher than he was. But that didn't matter. Benno came cheap. He hadn't cost Massino much and the suckers of the town were impressed by his battered face, the way he walked and spat on the sidewalk. They thought he was real tough and that was what Massino wanted them to think. With Benno locked in the office, with Massino's reputation and that great hunk of safe, the suckers who parted with their money felt sure that when they came to pay-out day, the money would be there, waiting for them.

Johnny knew all this. The opening of the safe and Benno presented no problem. He remembered what Massino had said: *No one would have the guts to touch anything that belonged to me.*

Well, Johnny was going to touch something that belonged to Massino. Guts? Probably not, but the urge to get his hands on such a sum, the smell of the sea, the dream of a beautiful thirty-footer added up to a lot more than guts. A grave-digger? There would be no grave-digger if his planning was right, Johnny told himself.

The big safe remained empty all the week. It was only on Friday that it was used. There was no combination; just a heavy old-fashioned key. During the months, Johnny, passing by Andy's open door, got to know the key was often left in the lock. On Friday when the take was put in the safe, Andy took the key home with him. Three times, long after midnight, Johnny had entered the building, gone up to Andy's office, picked the door lock and had hunted for the key. Third time lucky! On a Wednesday night, he had found the key in the safe. He had come prepared with a lump of softened putty. The impression had taken only a few seconds, but God! how he had sweated!

No one was ever allowed inside Andy's office. If someone wanted to speak to him that someone stayed in the doorway and did his talking but never crossed the threshold. Andy had a thing about this. The only exception was when Benno guarded the safe on Friday nights, then Andy would clear his desk, lock every drawer and generally behave as if vermin was invading his holy of holies.

It took Johnny three nights to make the key, then on the fourth night he returned to the building, again picking the door lock to Andy's office and tried out his handiwork. A touch with a file, a drop of oil and the key worked perfectly.

Taking the money was now easy. Even fixing Benno wasn't too tricky. It was what happened when Massino found he had been robbed that mattered.

There's no one dumb enough to try to take anything from me.

The trick in this steal, Johnny had decided, was not to let Massino find out who had taken the money. Once Massino knew who the thief was, that thief had as much chance of surviving as a scoop of ice cream dropped into a furnace.

17

Massino was affiliated with the Mafia to whom he paid regular dues. His own organization could take care of the town: he would get away as fast as he could. So Massino would call his opposite Mafia number and alert him. The whole of the Mafia organization would swing into action. No one steals from the Mafia or its friends without paying for it: that was a matter of principle. There wouldn't be a town nor a city in the whole country that would be safe. Johnny knew all this, and his plan was to fix things so that no one could guess who had taken the money.

He had thought about this a lot as his future and his life depended on it. When he had the money, he would rush it across the street to the Greyhound left-luggage lockers and dump it there. The money would stay there until the heat cooled off – probably three or four weeks. Then when he was sure Massino was convinced whoever had grabbed the money had got away with it, he (Johnny) would move the money to a safe-deposit bank. He wished he could do this as soon as he had the money, but his alibi depended on speed. The Greyhound bus station was right opposite Massino's office. It would be only a matter of minutes to dump the bag and get back to Melanie's pad. The safe-deposit bank was at the other end of the town and anyway it would be shut for the night.

The whole operation involved great patience. Once the money was in the safe-deposit bank, Johnny knew he would have to wait two or three years, but he could wait, knowing when he left town he would have all that money to set up somewhere in Florida, get his boat and achieve his ambition. What were two or three years after waiting all this time?

Massino had the police in his pocket. Johnny knew the police would be called in once the robbery was discovered and they would go over the safe and Andy's office for fingerprints. That didn't worry Johnny. He would wear gloves and have an unassailable alibi: he would be in bed with Melanie during the time of the steal with his car parked outside her pad. He knew he could rely on Melanie to cover those thirty minutes when he was making the steal.

Because the safe had been obviously opened by a key, the full weight of Massino's suspicions would fall on Andy, and the police would really take Andy to the cleaners since he had the only key and had a criminal record. Maybe Andy wouldn't be able to clear himself, but if he did, then Massino would look around at the other members of his mob. He would know it was an inside job because of the key. He had two hundred men who came and went. The last man, Johnny told himself, he would suspect was his faithful Johnny who had saved his life three times in the past, had always behaved himself and had always done as he was told.

Sitting there before the window, Johnny went over the plan again and again and he couldn't fault it and yet he was uneasy.

He could hear Massino's harsh, ruthless voice saying: *There's no one dumb enough to try to take anything from me.*

But there could be someone smart enough, Johnny thought and putting his fingers inside his shirt, he touched the St Christopher medal.

2

Melanie Carelli, Johnny's girl, had been born in a Naples slum. At the age of four she had been sent out on to the streets with other kids to beg from the tourists. Life had been hard for her and also for her parents. Her father, a cripple, had touted postcards, and faked Parker pens outside the better class hotels; her mother had taken in washing.

When Melanie reached the age of fifteen, her grandfather, who had a tailoring business in Brooklyn, wrote to say he could use her in his tiny factory and her mother and father were glad to see her go: the steerage fare provided for by her grandfather. Melanie was too keen on the boys and her parents dreaded the almost certain prospect that sooner or later she would land them with an unwanted baby.

For three soul-destroying years she had worked in the factory and finally decided this wasn't going to be her way of life. She stole fifty dollars from her grandfather and left Brooklyn. Arriving at East City, Johnny's town, she decided it was far enough away from New York to be safe and she settled there. She had no need to worry about safety: her grandfather was only too happy to find her missing.

She got a job as a waitress in a sleazy snack bar, but the hours were killing. She quitted and other jobs followed, then after a year she finally got taken on in one of the many cheap stores in town which suited her. The pay wasn't much, but at least she was on her own with no one to tell her what to do or how to behave and she had a tiny room that belonged to her, and to her only.

Melanie was sexually attractive without being pretty. She had long, coal-black hair, large breasts and solid hips and the hot sun of Naples in her loins. Men, looking at her, knew it. The store buyer, a timid, fat man, living in terror of his wife, became infatuated with her. She allowed him from time to time to put his hand up her skirt, but no more, and in return he put her in charge of the men's shirt counter with a raise in pay.

It was while Johnny Bianda was buying shirts that he became aware of her. At that moment, he was without a girl, having quarrelled with a pick-up who had been too exacting, and he was in need of a girl. As always, Melanie was in need of a man. He dated her for dinner, proved he was generous and for the past three years, they had been going steady.

Within two months of meeting Johnny, Melanie moved out of her tiny room and into a two-room apartment in a walk-up, Johnny providing the rent and the furnishing.

In spite of being grateful and liking Johnny, Melanie regretted that he was so much older than she, that he was bulky and far from glamorous, but he treated her right, was nice to her and always had money to spend on her. They met three times a week: sometimes he would take her out to dinner and then to a movie, sometimes she would cook Italian food for him at home. Whatever the programme, they always finished up on the big double bed that Johnny had bought for her, and it was then, after so much experience with younger men, that she really appreciated Johnny as a lover. He and no one else could satisfy her.

To Johnny, Melanie, although so much younger than he and with no thoughts in her head, was a girl he felt he could trust and this was important to him. He was sick of the diggers, the cheats and the toughies with whom he had previously associated. Melanie came as a breath of fresh air. To him, she was more than attractive: she was wildly eager in bed and she didn't yak as all those other women had yakked. She would be content to sit by his side in silence or talk when he was in the mood, and she never hinted of marriage.

Johnny felt in his bones he would never marry. He didn't want a permanent woman: all he wanted was a boat and the sea and sex when the mood was on him. Sooner or later, he knew he would lose Melanie. Some young punk with a little money would come along and that would be that. Because he knew he would eventually lose her, he had never told her about his urge to own a boat, and now he was committed to the steal, he was thankful he hadn't told her: that he had told no one. Massino was an expert at squeezing information from anyone when he wanted and if the steal turned sour and Massino even suspected it was he (Johnny) who had taken the money he would brutally quizz everyone connected with Johnny. If Massino ever got the idea that Johnny was boat mad, it would be goodbye to the boat.

Most of Massino's mob knew that Johnny's girl was Melanie. You can't take a girl out three times a week for three years without running into some of the mob at the restaurants Johnny could afford nor at a movie house showing the latest film. This thought worried Johnny a little, although he kept assuring himself that nothing would turn sour the way he had planned the steal and that Massino would never suspect he was the thief. He was fond of Melanie. Love? No, he told himself, he wasn't in love with her. He felt that love didn't come into his life. Love bound a man, but he was fond of her and wouldn't want anything to happen to her.

He lit another cigarette. In the street below a child yelled, a woman called across the street to another woman, the car crawled by in low gear, making a racket of noise. Listening to the noise, he thought of the sea in the sunshine and felt the breeze against his face. His hands closed on the spokes of the tiller and he heard the murmur of the powerful engines. Patience, he told himself. Two or three years and he would be afloat.

Every Friday night he took Melanie out to dinner and then to a movie. This night – he glanced at his watch – he would be taking her out. Next Friday would be different, but he wouldn't tell her tonight. He would jump it on her. Although she wasn't a talker, if she knew beforehand that next Friday was going to be special, she might worry.

He spent the next two hours going over his plan again and again, then finally, realizing the futility of this constant rehashing, he got up, stripped off and took a shower.

An hour later he picked Melanie up outside her apartment and drove her to Luigi's restaurant.

They had a good Italian dinner. They didn't have much to say to each other. Melanie always seemed to be hungry and when the food was placed before her, she ate happily and in silence while Johnny, now thinking of Friday 29th, pushed his food around on the plate and didn't eat much. He kept looking at her. His eyes took away her clothes and saw her olive-skinned, lush body naked and he thought of the wasted three hours ahead of them when they would sit in a stuffy movie house and watch some goddamn film before he could lay her on her back on the big double bed.

"Have you something on your mind, Johnny?" Melanie asked suddenly. She had devoured an enormous plate of spaghetti and was sitting back, eager for the next course, her big breasts forcing themselves against her cheap skimpy dress.

Johnny jerked his thoughts back to her and he smiled.

"Just looking at you, baby," he said and put his hand over hers. "Right now, I've got the hots for you."

She felt a hot rush of blood to her loins.

"Me too. Let's skip the movie tonight. Let's go back and have a real ball."

That was what he wanted and his fingers closed tightly over the back of her hand.

"You have yourself a deal, baby."

Then a shadow fell across the table and Johnny looked up. Toni Capello was standing there. He was wearing a black suit, a yellow-and-white striped shirt and a yellow kipper tie. He looked very dressy, but his flat snake's eyes remained snake's eyes.

"Hi, Johnny," he said and his eyes shifted to Melanie and then back to Johnny. "The boss wants you."

Johnny turned hot with anger. He knew Toni was almost as good as he was (had been?) with a gun and he hated Toni as he knew Toni hated him.

He sensed Melanie was scared. He glanced at her and saw she was looking at Toni with wide, frightened eyes.

"What do you mean ... he wants me?" Johnny demanded. A waiter hovered to change the plates, then moved away.

"Like I said ... he wants you and pronto."

Johnny drew in a long deep breath.

"Okay. I'll be along. Where?"

"At his place and right now. I'll take the doll back to her pad." Toni smirked. "A pleasure."

"Get the hell out of here, you cheap punk," Johnny said quietly and dangerously. "I'll be there, but in my time."

Toni sneered.

"Okay, if you want to cut your throat ... that's fine with me. I'll tell the boss," and he walked out of the restaurant.

Melanie turned, her eyes wide.

"What is it, Johnny?"

He wished he knew. He had never been called to Massino's house before. He felt cold sweat start out on his forehead.

"Sorry, baby," he said gently. "I have to go. Suppose you finish your dinner, then take a taxi home and wait for me."

"Oh, no! I ..."

He got up and was moving around the table.

"Do it, baby, to please me," he said, a hard note creeping into his voice.

There was something now about him that frightened her. He had lost colour, seemed to have shrunk a little and there were sweat beads on his forehead.

She forced a smile.

"Okay, Johnny, I'll be waiting for you."

He had a word with the waiter and slipped him a bill, then giving her a wave, he went out on to the street.

It took him some twenty minutes in the heavy traffic to reach Massino's house on 10th street. He found parking with difficulty and walked up the marble steps leading to the massive front door.

While he had been driving, his mind had been racing. What in God's name, he wondered, did Massino want him for at this hour? Never before had he been summoned to this opulent house. He rang the bell, and as he was wiping his sweating hands on his handkerchief, the door opened and a lean, hard-faced man wearing a tail coat and a winged collar (for God's sake!) aping an English butler from the old movies, stood aside to let Johnny enter the vast hall, lined on either side with oil paintings in gilt frames and several suits of polished armour.

"Go ahead, bud," the butler said out of the side of his mouth. "First door right."

Johnny entered a large room, lined with books and full of heavy dark furniture. Joe Massino was lounging in a big wing chair, smoking a cigar, a glass of whisky and water at his elbow. Sitting in the shadows was Ernie Lassini, picking his teeth with a splinter of wood.

"Come on in, Johnny," Massino said. "Sit down." He waved to a chair opposite him. "What'll you drink?"

Johnny sat down stiffly.

"A whisky will do fine, thank you," he said.

"Ernie, get Johnny a whisky and then get your ass out of here."

There was a long pause while Ernie fixed the drink which he handed to Johnny, his fat, scarred face dead pan, then he left the room.

"Cigar?" Massino asked.

"No, thanks, Mr Joe."

Massino grinned.

"Did I interrupt something?"

"Yeah." Johnny stared at the big man. "You sure did."

Massino laughed, then leaning forward he slapped Johnny on his knee.

"It'll keep. She'll be all the more eager when you get to her."

Johnny didn't say anything. Holding the drink in his sweating hand, he waited.

Massino stretched out his thick legs, drew on his cigar and puffed smoke to the ceiling. He looked very relaxed and amiable, but Johnny didn't relax. He had seen Massino in this mood before. It could change into snarling rage in seconds.

"Nice little pad I've got here, huh?" Massino said, looking around the room. "The wife fixed it up. All these goddamn books. She reckons they look fancy. You ever read a book, Johnny?"

"No."

"Nor do I. Who the hell wants to read a book?" The little cold grey eyes moved over Johnny. "Well, never mind that. I've been thinking about you, Johnny. You've worked for me close on twenty years ... correct?"

Here it is, Johnny thought. The kiss-off. Well, he had been expecting it, but not quite as soon as this.

"I guess it's around twenty years," he said.

"What do I pay you, Johnny?"

"Two hundred a week."

"That's what Andy tells me. Yeah ... two hundred. You should have squawked long before now."

"I'm not squawking," Johnny said quietly. "I guess a guy gets paid what he deserves."

Massino squinted at him.

"That's not the way these other punks think. They're always moaning for more money." He drank some of his whisky, paused, then went on, "You're my best man, Johnny. There's something in you that gets to me. Maybe I remember your shooting. I wouldn't be here with all these fancy goddamn books around me if it hadn't been for you ... three times, wasn't it?"

"Yeah."

27

"Three times." Massino shook his head. "Some shooting." Again a long pause, then he said, "If you had come to me two ... three years ago and said you wanted more money, I'd have given it to you." The red tip of his cigar suddenly pointed at Johnny. "Why didn't you?"

"I've told you, Mr Joe," Johnny said. "A guy gets paid what he deserves. I don't do much. I work off and on. Friday is the big day ... so ... "

"You and Sammy get along okay?"

"Sure."

"He's scared. He hates the job, doesn't he?"

"He needs the money."

"That's right. I'm thinking of making a change. I've had a beef or two from the boys. Times change. They don't seem to like a smoke picking up the money. I want your angle. Do you think I should make a change?"

Johnny's mind moved swiftly. This was no time to support anyone, even Sammy. In another six days – if it worked out – he would have something like $150,000 hidden away.

"I walk it with Sammy," he said woodenly. "That's been my job for ten years, Mr Joe. I'll walk it with anyone you pick."

"I'm thinking of making a complete change," Massino said. "You and Sammy. Ten years is a hell of a time. Can Sammy drive a car?"

"Sure and he knows cars. He started life in a garage."

"I heard that. Think he'd like to be my chauffeur? The wife has been nagging me. She says it isn't good class for me to drive the Rolls. She wants a uniform for God's sake! She thinks Sammy would look real good in a uniform."

"You can but ask him, Mr Joe."

"You talk to him, Johnny. What does he get paid?"

"A hundred."

"Okay, tell him it's worth a hundred and fifty."

"I'll tell him."

Again a long pause while Johnny waited to hear his own fate.

"Now you, Johnny," Massino said. "You're a well known character in this town. People like and respect you. You've got a reputation. How would you like to take over the one-arm bandits?"

Johnny stiffened. This was the last thing he expected to be offered ... the last thing he wanted. Bernie Schultz, a fat, ageing man, looked after these gambling machines for Massino: had looked after them for the past five years. He had often moaned to Johnny about his worries, how Andy was continually chasing him if the take from these machines fell below what Bernie declared was an impossible weekly target.

He remembered Bernie, sweating, dark rings around his eyes, saying, "The goddamn job isn't worth it, Johnny. You've no idea. You're always under pressure from that sonofabitch to find new outlets. You walk your goddamn feet off, trying to get creeps to take the machines. Then if they take them, some goddamn kid busts them. You never stop working."

"How about Bernie?" Johnny asked to gain time.

"Bernie's washed up." Massino's amiable expression changed and he now became the cold, ruthless executive. "You can handle this, Johnny. You won't have trouble in finding new outlets. People respect you. It'll be worth four hundred and a one per cent cut: could net you eight hundred if you really got stuck into the job. What do you say?"

29

Johnny thought swiftly. This was an offer he dare not refuse. He was sure if he did, he would be out and he wasn't yet ready to be kissed off.

Looking straight at Massino, he said, "When do I start?" Massino grinned and, leaning forward, he slapped Johnny's knee.

"That's the way I like a guy to talk," he said. "I knew I'd picked the right one. You start the first of the month. I'll have Bernie fixed by then. You talk it over with Andy. He'll wise you up." He got to his feet, looked at his watch and grimaced. "I've got to move along. Got to take the wife to some goddamn shindig. Well, okay, Johnny, that's a deal. You've got yourself eight hundred bucks a week." He put his heavy arm around Johnny's shoulders and led him to the door. "Talk to Sammy. If he wants the job, tell him to see Andy who will fix his uniform. You two do the next collection and then you start your new jobs ... right?"

"That's fine with me," Johnny said and moved out into the big hall where the butler was waiting.

"See you," Massino said and strode up the stairs, whistling under his breath and out of Johnny's sight.

*　　*　　*

Reaching his car, Johnny stood hesitating. He looked at his watch. The time was 21.05. Knowing Melanie's eating capacity he guessed she would be occupied for another half hour. He decided it might pay off to have a word with Bernie Schultz.

He drove across town and reached Bernie's apartment in fifteen minutes. He found Bernie at home, his shoes off, a beer in his hand, watching TV.

Bernie's wife, a big, fat happy-faced woman let him in and then went into the kitchen because she knew these two were going to talk business and she never mixed herself up in any of Bernie's machinations.

Johnny didn't hedge.

As soon as Bernie had turned off the TV and offered beer which Johnny refused, Johnny said, "I've just talked with Mr Joe. You're getting the kiss off, Bernie, and I'm getting your job."

Bernie stared at him.

"Come again?"

Johnny repeated what he had said.

"You really mean that ... no kidding?"

"I'm telling you."

Bernie drew in a long, deep breath and his heavy, fat face lit up with a broad grin. Suddenly, he looked ten years younger.

"Is that great news!" He clapped his hands together. "I've been praying for this for years! So, now I'm free!"

"I guessed you would feel that way," Johnny said. "That's why I came right over. What'll you do, Bernie? You'll be out of the organization."

"Do? Me?" Bernie laughed happily. "I've got money put by. My brother-in-law owns a fruit farm in California. That's where I'll be: partners, picking fruit in the sun with not a goddamn care in the world!"

"Yeah." Johnny's mind shifted to his dream boat and the sea. "Well, I've got your job, Bernie. What's it worth?"

Bernie finished his beer, belched and set down the glass.

"Mr Joe pays me a flat eight hundred a week and one per cent of the take, but the one per cent means nothing. All the goddamn years I've worked, I've never reached the target above that sonofabitch Andy's target, so you can forget the

31

one per cent. But you get paid eight hundred steady, Johnny, although the job is sheer hell. I've managed to save out of what I got paid and you can too."

Eight hundred a week and Massino had offered him only four hundred and one per cent which according to Bernie meant nothing!

A cold, fierce rage took hold of Johnny, but he controlled it.

You're my best man, Johnny. There's something in you that gets to me.

That's what the thieving, double-crossing sonofabitch had said! Well, okay, Johnny thought as he got to his feet, I'll be a thieving sonofabitch too!

Leaving Bernie, he went down to where he had parked his car. Still raging, he drove fast to Melanie's pad.

* * *

The following morning when Melanie had gone to work, Johnny returned to his apartment and cooked himself breakfast which was his favourite meal. He had the whole day before him with no plans. He was in a surly mood. Massino's meanness still irked him. He had now no misgivings about robbing him, that was for sure.

As he was sitting down to three fried eggs and a thick slice of grilled ham, the telephone bell rang. Cursing, he got up and lifted the receiver. It was Andy Lucas on the line.

"Mr Joe says you're to take over Bernie's job," Andy said. "You two had better get together. See him today. He'll take you around with him and give you introductions."

"Okay," Johnny said, eyeing his breakfast. "I'll do that."

"And listen, Johnny." Andy's voice was cold. "Bernie has been lying down on the job. I'll expect you to increase the business. We want at least two hundred more machines out and that'll be your job ... understand?"

"Sure."

"Okay ... go talk to Bernie," and Andy hung up.

Johnny returned to his breakfast but he hadn't the appetite he had had before the telephone call.

A little after 11.00, he went out and headed for Bernie's office: a one-room affair on the top floor of a walk-up office block. As he was waiting for the traffic lights to change so he could cross the road, he saw Sammy the Black waiting to cross on the other side of the street.

Sammy grinned and waved and when the traffic stopped, Johnny joined him.

"Hi, Sammy ... what are you doing?"

"Me?" Sammy looked vague. "Not a thing, Mr Johnny. Not much doing on Saturday... just mooching around."

Johnny had forgotten it was Saturday. Tomorrow would be Sunday. He hated Sundays with the shops shut and people going out of town. Usually he spent Sunday mornings reading the papers and then joining Melanie in the late afternoon. Sunday morning she was always busy, cleaning her apartment, washing her hair and doing all the goddamn chores women seem to find to do.

"Want coffee?" Johnny asked.

"Always say yes to coffee." Sammy looked uneasily at Johnny. The hard expression on Johnny's face bothered him. "Something wrong?"

"Let's have coffee." Johnny led the way to the café and propped himself up against the bar. He ordered the coffees, then said, "I was talking to Mr Joe last night." He went on to tell Sammy what Massino had said. "It's up to you. Do you want to drive his car?"

Sammy's face lit up as if he had swallowed a lighted electric light bulb.

"Is this straight, Mr Johnny?"

"That's what he said."

"Sure do!" Sammy slapped his pink palms together. "You mean I don't have to collect any more money?"

Johnny thought sourly: another one! Bernie, beaming from ear to ear, now Sammy. They have it smooth while I get it rough.

"You have to wear a uniform and drive his Rolls. Like the idea?"

"Sure do! Is this good news!" Sammy paused then looked at Johnny. "When do I start?"

"The week after next." Sammy's face fell.

"You mean I've got the collection next Friday to do?"

"That's right."

Sammy's eyes rolled and sweat broke out on his face.

"Couldn't the new man do the job, Mr Johnny? Who's the new man anyway?"

"I wouldn't know. We make the collection together on the 29th, Sammy." Johnny finished his coffee. "So forget it."

"Yes." Sammy blotted his sweating face with his handkerchief. "You think it'll be all right."

"Can't go wrong." Johnny moved away from the bar. "I've things to do. Go see Andy. Tell him you'll drive for Mr Joe. He'll fix everything. It pays a hundred and fifty."

Sammy's eyes opened wide.

"A hundred and fifty?"

"That's what Mr Joe said." Johnny looked thoughtfully at Sammy. "Are you still keeping your savings under your bed?"

"Where else should I keep it, Mr Johnny?"

34

"I told you, you dope, in a goddamn bank!"

"I wouldn't do that," Sammy said, shaking his head. "Banks are for white people."

Johnny shrugged.

"Be seeing you." He paid for the coffees and walked out of the café. Ten minutes later he was in Bernie Schultz's office.

Bernie was resting behind his battered desk, his chair pushed back, his thumbs hooked to his belt.

When he saw Johnny, he straightened up.

"Andy said I was to look in," Johnny said. "He said you'd give me introductions and take me around."

"Sure will," Bernie said, "but not today. This is the weekend for God's sake! No business at weekends. Suppose we start Monday, huh? Come here around ten o'clock. I'll show you around. Okay?"

"Anything you say." Johnny started towards the door.

"Oh, Johnny ..."

Johnny paused and looked at Bernie who was scratching his fat jowl.

"Yeah?"

"I guess I flapped with my big mouth." Bernie shifted uneasily in his chair. "Andy told me I wasn't to tell you what I get paid. Can you forget it?"

Johnny's hands turned to fists, but he managed a cold grin.

"Sure. I've forgotten it, Bernie. See you Monday," and he left the little office and tramped down the six flights of stairs, swearing under his breath.

As he was within a five-minute walk from the Greyhound bus station, he made his way there. Reaching the station, he paused to look across the street and up at Massino's office windows. Massino was probably in flight to Miami for a long weekend, but Johnny was sure that Andy was up there in his poky office.

He went into the bus station and made his way to the left luggage lockers. He stopped to read the instructions printed on the door of one of the lockers. The key, he read, had to be collected from the attendant. He glanced around. Seeing no one among the milling crowd he knew, he wandered over to the attendant's cubby hole. A big, sleepy-looking negro peered at him.

"Let's have a key," Johnny said. "How much?"

"How long do you want it for, boss?"

"Three weeks ... maybe longer. I don't know."

The negro handed over the key.

"Half a buck a week: that'll be a buck and a half for three weeks."

Johnny paid, dropped the key into his pocket, then went to locate the locker. It was conveniently placed: just inside the entrance door. Satisfied, he walked out into the cold and made his way back to his apartment.

He spent the next hour, sitting before his window, thinking of Massino. Around 14.00 just when he was thinking of getting a snack for lunch the telephone bell rang.

Grimacing, he got to his feet and lifted the receiver.

"Johnny?"

"Hi, baby!" He was surprised that Melanie should be calling. He had arranged to take her for a drive on Sunday afternoon and then spend the night with her.

"I've got the curse, Johnny. It started just now," Melanie said. "I'm feeling like hell. Can we forget tomorrow?"

Women! Johnny thought. Always something wrong! But he knew Melanie really suffered when she had her period. This would mean a long, lonely, dreary weekend for him.

"Sorry about that, baby," he said gently. "Sure, we'll forget tomorrow. There'll be plenty of other Sundays. Anything I can do?"

"Nothing. As soon as I get home, I'll go to bed. It doesn't last all that long."

"You want any food?"

"I'll take in something. You have a nice time, Johnny. I'll call you as soon as it's over and then we'll have fun."

"Yeah. Well, look after yourself," and Johnny hung up. He wandered around the room wondering what the hell he would do over the weekend. He took out his wallet and checked his money. He had one hundred and eight dollars of his pay left. This would have to last him until next Friday. He hesitated. It would be good to get in his car and drive down to the coast: a three hundred mile drive. He could put up at a motel and walk by the sea, but it would cost. He couldn't afford that kind of weekend. Fine for Massino who had all the money in the world, but strictly not for Johnny Bianda.

Shrugging, he crossed over to the TV set and turned it on. He sat down before the screen and gave himself over, with bored indifference, to a ball game.

As he watched, his mind dwelt on the time when he would be on his boat, feeling the lift and fall of the deck, feeling the spray of the sea against his face and the heat of the sun.

Patience, he told himself, patience.

3

Johnny came awake with a start and looked at his strap watch, then he relaxed. The time was 06.30 ... plenty of time, he told himself and he looked at Melanie, sleeping by his side. Her long black hair half covered her face and she was making a soft snorting sound as she slept.

Cautiously, not to disturb her, he reached for his pack of cigarettes on the bedside table, lit up and dragged smoke gratefully into his lungs.

Today, he told himself was D-day: Friday 29th. The collection began at 10.00. By 15.00 he and Sammy would have collected something like $150,000! The Big Take! In eighteen hours' time, if he had any luck, all this money would be his and safely stashed away in a Greyhound luggage locker.

If he had any luck.

He fingered the St Christopher medal lying on his bare chest. He thought of his mother: *as long as you wear it, nothing really bad can happen to you.*

Lying still, he recalled the past days that had slipped away so quickly. On Monday, he had gone the rounds with Bernie, meeting people, hearing them yak, looking for new sites for the one-arm bandits. To Bernie's startled amazement, Johnny had placed five machines in new locations on his first day. As usual, Massino had made the right choice in picking Johnny. Most people, living in the

City, knew Johnny by reputation: a tough, hard man and good with a gun. When he walked into some café and looked directly at the owner, suggesting in his quiet voice that the owner could do with one of Massino's gambling machines, there was no argument.

Even Andy had been pleased when Johnny's total for four days had been eighteen machines placed in new locations.

Now here was Friday 29th. One more collection and he would then move into the world of one-arm bandits and Bernie would gratefully bow out. These past four days had told Johnny that the job wasn't all that bad. Unlike Bernie, he had the reputation behind him to wave in people's faces: he realized no one respected Bernie and he marvelled that Bernie had lasted as long as he had.

Johnny touched off the ash of his cigarette as he stared up at the ceiling. He was relieved that he had no qualms, no feeling of nerves. He thought of all that money: $150,000! He mustn't be too successful with the one-arm bandits, he warned himself. He wanted to retire from the scene in two years. He could wait that long, but no longer. His first year would be good. Maybe, he might even qualify for the one per cent deal, but the following year, he would slow down, appearing to lose his grip, and knowing Massino and Andy, they would look around for a younger man. Then he could bow out as Bernie was now bowing out.

Melanie stirred and half sat up.

"You want coffee, honey?" she asked sleepily.

He stubbed out his cigarette and leaned over her.

"There's time." His fingers caressed her breast and she sighed happily.

Later, when they were having breakfast, Johnny said casually, "I'll see you tonight, baby. We'll go to Luigi's."

Melanie, happily eating pancakes and syrup, nodded.

"Yes, Johnny."

He paused, not quite sure how to tell her. Goddamn it! He thought, this can't be complicated. Tell her half the truth. She'll buy anything ... just half the truth.

"Baby, I have a job to do tonight," he said as he cut into his pancake. "Are you listening?"

She looked up. The syrup was making a tiny trickle down her chin.

"Yes."

"This job is nothing to do with my boss and he wouldn't want me to do it. It means a little more money for me, but Massino mustn't know about it." He paused and looked at her. She was listening. Her black eyes were already showing signs of panic. She had always been terrified of Massino and hated Johnny working for him. "There's nothing to worry about," he went on, his voice soft and soothing. "You know what an alibi means?"

She put down her knife and fork and nodded.

"I need an alibi, baby, and I want you to supply it. Now listen, tonight, we eat at Luigi's, then we come here. I leave my car outside. Around midnight, I'll leave you for thirty minutes while I do this job. I come back and if any questions are asked you say I didn't leave you once we got back after dinner. Get it?"

Melanie put her hands to her face and her elbows on the table. It was a bad sign, Johnny told himself that she had now lost interest in her food.

"What job?" she asked.

He too suddenly didn't want anything more to eat. He pushed his plate aside and lit a cigarette.

"That's something you needn't know, baby," he said. "It's a job. All you have to tell anyone who might ask is that we spent the night here together and I didn't leave you for a second. Will you do that?"

She stared at him, her soft black eyes frightened.

"Who will ask?"

"The chances are no one will ask, baby." He forced a smile. "But maybe the fuzz will ask ... maybe Massino."

She flinched.

"I don't want trouble, Johnny. No ... don't ask me to do it."

He pushed back his chair and stood up. He had half expected this reaction, knowing Melanie as he did. He moved to the window and looked down at the slow-moving traffic. He was sure of her. She would do it, he told himself, but she needed to be persuaded.

He let a long silence build up, then turning, he came back to the table and sat down.

"I've never asked you to do anything for me, have I? Not once. I've done a lot for you. You have this apartment, the furniture, you have lots of things I have given you, but never once have I ever asked you to do anything for me ... now, I'm asking. It's important."

She stared at him.

"I just have to say that you were here tonight and you didn't leave?"

"That's it. You say after we had dinner at Luigi's we came back here and I didn't leave here until eight o'clock in the morning. Get it? I didn't move from here from ten tonight until eight tomorrow."

Melanie looked down at her cold pancake.

"Well, if it's so important, I guess I could say that," she said doubtfully.

"That's fine." He wished he could convey to her how important it was. "So, okay, you'll do it?"

41

"I don't like doing it, but I'll do it."

He ran his fingers through his hair, trying to control his exasperation.

"Baby, this is serious. The fuzz could yell at you. You know how the fuzz act. You must stick with this. Even if Massino bawls at you, you must stick with this ... Do you understand?"

"Must I do it, Johnny? I'd rather not."

He fondled her hand, trying to instil confidence in her.

"You'll be repaying a debt, baby. Don't you want to help me?"

She stared at him for a long moment, her eyes showing her fear, then she put her other hand over his and gripped it hard.

"Okay, Johnny... I'll do it."

And he knew by the tone of her voice she would do it and he relaxed.

He got to his feet and she came around the table to press herself against him. His hand slid up under her nightdress and cupped her heavy buttocks.

"I've got to get moving, baby," he said. "See you tonight. Don't worry ... it's nothing, baby ... just a little lie."

Leaving her, he ran down the stairs and to where he had parked his car. Ten minutes later, he was back in his apartment. He shaved and showered. As he stood under the cold water, he wondered if Melanie would have the guts to face Massino if things turned sour. Maybe she would. He touched his St Christopher medal. The trick with this steal was not to let Massino nor the fuzz even suspect who had taken the money.

He drove up to Massino's office, arriving there a few minutes to 10.00. Toni Capello and Ernie Lassini were already there, propping up a wall in the office, smoking. Sammy came up the stairs as Johnny entered the office.

"Hi!" Johnny paused. "The big day. You got your uniform fixed?"

Sammy's face was already glistening with sweat. There was a grey tinge under the black of his skin. Johnny could see he was scared to death and he knew Sammy's panic would grow as the collection went on.

"Mr Andy's fixing it," Sammy said huskily and moved into the office.

Toni and Ernie greeted them. The four men stood around for some minutes, then Andy came from his office with two collection bags. They were handcuffed together and there was a spare handcuff which Andy snapped on Sammy's wrist and which was attached to one of the bags.

Toni said, "I wouldn't have your job for a thousand bucks." He was grinning, seeing Sammy's fear. "Man! Could some guy take a swing at your wrist with an axe!"

"Cut it out!" Johnny snapped, his voice dangerous. "No one's swinging no axes."

There was a sudden silence as Massino came into the office.

"All set?" Massino asked Andy.

"They're on their way."

"Well ..." Massino grinned at Johnny. "So ..."

Johnny waited, his face expressionless.

"Last round-up, huh?" Massino said. "You're going to do fine with the bandits, Johnny." He looked at Sammy. "You're going to do fine as my chauffeur. Okay, get moving. The Big Take!" He went to his desk and sat down.

As Toni and Ernie, followed by Sammy, moved to the door, Massino said, "Johnny?"

Johnny paused.

"You got that goddamn medal on?" Massino was grinning.

"I'm never without it, Mr Joe."

Massino nodded.

"Watch it! You could need it on this trip."

"We three will be watching it, Mr Joe," Johnny said quietly.

The four men left the office and walked down the stairs to Johnny's car.

*   *   *

Five hours later, it was over. There had been no trouble. The police looked the other way when Johnny double parked, slowing the flow of traffic. Money rolled into the bags. Sammy, expecting to hear any second the bang of a gun and to feel a bullet smash into his body was almost gibbering by the time Johnny pulled up outside Massino's office block.

Johnny touched him on his shoulder.

"Finished," he said quietly. "Now the Rolls."

But Sammy still didn't feel safe. He had to cross the sidewalk, dragging the heavy bags before he finally reached the haven of Massino's office.

With Johnny at his side and Ernie and Toni, fanned out, their hands gripping their gun butts, he got out of the car and into the rain. He cringed at the crowd waiting around the entrance to the office block to cheer the four men as they arrived.

Then the blessed dimness of the lobby and the ride up in the elevator.

"How does it feel, boy, to be carrying all that dough?" Toni asked.

Sammy looked at him, then away. He was thinking that tomorrow he would be really safe, fitted with a grey uniform, wearing a peaked cap with a black cockade and at the wheel of a Corniche Rolls. After ten years of fear, he had come through without being shot at and without having his hand chopped off and now he was heading for pastures green.

With Johnny at his side, he shambled into Massino's office and set down the two heavy bags on Massino's desk.

Andy was there, waiting. Massino was chewing a dead cigar. As Andy unlocked the handcuff, Massino lifted his eyebrows at Johnny. It was a silent question: "No trouble?" Johnny shook his head.

Then came the ritual while Andy counted the money. It took some time. Finally, Andy looked at Massino and pursing his thin lips said, "This is the tops, Mr Joe: one hundred and eighty-six thousand. Some take!"

Johnny felt a rush of hot blood down his spine. The jackpot! In a few hours this enormous sum of money would be his! A thirty-footer? He would now be able to make new plans. A forty-five-footer now came into his mind.

He watched Andy tug the two bags into his office and after a moment or so, he heard the old-fashioned safe door clang shut.

Massino took from his desk drawer a bottle of Johnny Walker. Ernie produced glasses. Massino poured himself a generous shot, then offered the bottle to Johnny.

"Go ahead," Massino said. "You're my boy, Johnny. Twenty years! I wanted you to be in on the biggest take." He leaned back, grinning. "Now, you've got a career ahead of you."

Ernie poured the rest of the drinks. Sammy refused. There was a pause while the men toasted themselves, then the telephone bell started up and Massino waved them away.

As Johnny and Sammy walked down the stairs, Sammy said, "It's been tough, Mr Johnny and I'm sorry you and me won't work together no more. You've been good to me. You've helped me. I want to say thanks."

"Let's go drink beer," Johnny said and as he walked into the rain, he felt the spray of the sea against his face and the lurch of a forty-five-footer beneath his feet.

They drank beer in the dimness of Freddy's bar.

"I guess this is goodbye, Sammy," Johnny said as Sammy waved to the barman for a second round. "You see ... nothing ever happened all these years. You were scared about nothing."

"I guess." Sammy shook his head. "There are folk who always worry and folk who don't. You're lucky, Mr Johnny. You don't ever seem to worry."

Johnny thought of the steal. Worry? No! After all he was over forty: half way to death. Even if the steal turned sour, he could tell himself when the crunch came that at least he had tried to achieve an ambition. But the steal wasn't going to turn sour. There would be no crunch.

Out in the rain, the two men – one white, the other black – looked at each other. There was an awkward pause, then Johnny offered his hand.

"Well, so long, Sammy," he said. "We'll keep in touch."

They gripped hands.

"Keep saving your money," Johnny went on. "I'll be around. Anytime, anywhere if you want to yak ... you know."

Sammy's eyes grew misty.

"I know, Mr Johnny. I'm your friend ... remember, Mr Johnny. I'm your friend."

Johnny gave him a light punch on his chest, then walked away. As he walked he felt a shutter was closing down, cutting off a slice of his life. The clang of the shutter in his mind warned him that he was now even more out on his own.

Driving slowly, he reached his apartment at 17.20, climbed the stairs and let himself in. He felt in need of a drink, but he resisted it. No alcohol. He had to be sharp for this job: no whisky to make him feel reckless. He thought of the hours ahead: the dinner with Melanie: the slow creeping minutes. He went to the window and looked down on the narrow, traffic-congested street, then he stripped off and took a shower, put on his best suit and then looked at his watch. It was now 18.00. God! he thought, when waiting, how time crawled!

He checked the things he would need: a weighted rubber cosh, a folded newspaper, a pair of gloves, his cigarette lighter, the key to the safe and the left-luggage locker key. All these he laid out on the table. There was nothing else he needed except luck. He put his fingers inside his shirt and touched the St Christopher medal. In two years' time, he told himself, he would be at sea with the spokes of a tiller in his hands, steering a forty-five-footer into the bay with the sun on his face and the roar of powerful motors making the deck tremble.

Sitting before the window, he listened to the noise of the street floating up to him, the sound of the traffic and the kids yelling until the hands of his watch crawled to 19.30. Then he got to his feet, slid the cosh into his hip pocket, strapped on his gun harness, checked his .38, took the newspaper into the bathroom and damped it under the tap before putting it into his jacket pocket, put the two keys and the gloves in another pocket and he was ready to go.

He drove to Melanie's apartment, arriving there just on 20.00. She was waiting in the doorway and got into the car as Johnny pulled up.

"Hi, baby!" He tried to make his voice sound casual. "Everything okay?"

"Yes." Her tone was flat. He could see she was uneasy and he hoped to God she hadn't changed her mind.

The meal wasn't a success although Johnny extravagantly ordered lobster cocktails and turkey breasts done in hot chilli sauce. Neither of them did more than pick at the food. Johnny couldn't help thinking of the moment when he would have to tackle Benno. The business of rushing the two heavy bags across to the Greyhound station. He would have to leave the operation until after 02.00: between 02.00 and 03.00. Every thing depended on luck and putting down his fork, he touched the St Christopher medal through his shirt.

"I wish you would tell me what you are going to do, Johnny," Melanie said suddenly. She pushed her turkey away, only half eaten. "It worries me so. It's nothing bad, is it?"

"A job. Forget it, baby. You don't want to know anything about it ... it's the best way. You want coffee?"

"No."

"Let's go to a movie. Come on, baby, snap out of it. It's going to be all right."

Going to a movie was a good idea. It had grip and even Johnny forgot what he was going to do in a few hours' time. They returned to Melanie's apartment just after midnight and went up the stairs.

On the stairs, they ran into a girl who had an apartment opposite Melanie's. They paused to have a word. The girl knew Johnny and got on well with Melanie.

"Out of cigarettes!" she said. "My luck!"

This chance meeting pleased Johnny. Just in case anything turned sour, this girl could say he was with Melanie.

The girl went on down the stairs and Melanie and Johnny went on up. Johnny had left his car parked outside the entrance and the girl would see it.

"Want coffee?" Melanie asked, dropping her coat on the settee.

"A lot of it, baby." Johnny sat down. "I don't leave here for a couple of hours. I've got to stay awake."

After a while, she came back with a large pot of coffee, a cup and saucer which she set down on the table beside him.

"Thanks, baby, now you go to bed," Johnny said. "There's nothing to worry about. Go to bed ... go to sleep."

She stood hesitating, looking at him, then silently she went into the bedroom and shut the door. Johnny grimaced as he poured strong, black coffee into the cup.

He sat there, sipping coffee until 02.25, then he got to his feet and moving silently, he opened the bedroom door and looked into the darkness of the room.

"You going now?" Melanie asked out of the darkness, her voice quavering.

"Why aren't you asleep, for God's sake?"

"I can't sleep. I'm so worried, Johnny."

Women! he thought. Maybe he should have picked on someone else for his alibi. He shook his head in despair. What the hell was the matter with him? He wouldn't need an alibi! The way he had fixed this, Massino would never think he had taken the money.

"I'll be back in thirty minutes, baby. Take it easy... try to sleep," and he closed the door.

He left the apartment and walked down to the deserted street. Keeping in the shadows, he walked fast, heading for Massino's office.

It took him ten minutes of fast walking to reach the entrance of Massino's office block. He approached it from across the street and he saw a light on in Andy's office. That meant Benno was up there, either sleeping or smoking or doing some goddamn thing, while he kept watch.

Johnny looked to right and left. The street was deserted. He crossed the street, entered the dimly lit lobby and took the elevator to the fourth floor. Closing the elevator door gently, he walked up the two remaining flights to Massino's office.

The job had to be done fast so his alibi would stand up. Reaching the passage leading to Massino's and Andy's offices, he took out his handkerchief and removed the two electric light bulbs in the corridor. The stream of light coming through Andy's glazed door was enough for him to see. He took the newspaper from his pocket. It was still slightly damp. He paused for a moment to listen, then he crumpled the newspaper and put it down hard against Andy's office door. He lit his lighter and touched off the newspaper. Small flames made smoke. Johnny stood back, cosh in hand, and waited.

He didn't have to wait long. He heard a muttered curse, then the door was unlocked and Benno, squat, heavily built, stood in the doorway, gaping at the smouldering paper. Johnny waited, pressed against the wall.

Benno moved forward as Johnny knew he would. As he began to stamp on the smouldering newspaper, Johnny's cosh descended on the back of his head.

Johnny didn't pause to make certain he had put Benno away. He knew he had and there was no point in wasting seconds. He stepped to the safe, took the key from his pocket and opened the safe. He dragged out the two bags. Sweat was running down his face. The bags were a lot heavier than he had expected. Taking the safe key, carrying the bags, he stepped over Benno's inert body, paused for a brief moment to stamp out the smouldering newspaper, then thumbed the elevator button.

Descending to the ground floor, he looked cautiously into the deserted lobby, then carrying a bag in either gloved hand, he moved into the street. Again he paused, then satisfied he had the street to himself, he bolted across to the Greyhound bus station.

A big negro was sleepily brushing up and he didn't look at Johnny as he opened the locker. As Johnny heaved the bags into the locker, he heard a late bus start up and saw its headlights as it moved out onto the street. He had to shove hard to get the door shut. He turned the key, removed it and then walked out of the bus station.

The first move of the operation had jelled! He ducked down a side street and began to run. $186,000! There was a surge of triumph in him as he ran. It now couldn't turn sour! Massino would never suspect him! As he ran, he felt a strong, overpowering sexual need.

Darting through the back streets, deserted at this time of night, he finally reached Melanie's apartment block. He paused in the shadows, checking, making sure that no one was there to break his alibi, then moving fast, he entered the apartment block and took the elevator to Melanie's floor.

Again he paused in the elevator to make sure there was no one in the passage, then he darted across to Melanie's door, turned the handle and was in.

He leaned against the door. His heart thumping. Well, he had done it. He looked at his watch. The steal had taken twenty-five minutes!

"Johnny?"

Melanie, in her shortie nightdress, came into the living-room.

He forced a grin.

"Here I am ... like I said ... nothing to worry about."

She stared at him, her black eyes wide with fear.

"What happened?"

"I said not to worry." He took her in his arms. "But something's going to happen right now ... guess what?"

Picking her up, he carried her into the bedroom and laid her gently on the bed.

"It's okay, baby," he said, stripping off his jacket, dumping his gun harness and then pulling off his shirt. Maybe the tension of the past half hour was getting at him, but he wanted her as never before.

She lay still, staring at him.

"You and me ... this time it's going to be the best," he said as he was pulling the zipper of his trousers, he suddenly felt horribly naked. He stood motionless, looking down at her, feeling his raging desire for her like a flame hit by a bucketful of water.

"Your medal," Melanie said.

Johnny straightened. He looked down at his hairy chest.

The St Christopher medal no longer hung on its silver chain. With shaking hands he lifted the chain and saw the tiny hook that carried the medal was bent and open.

For the first time in his life, he felt a cold clutch of fear.

"Look for it!" The snap of his voice and the expression in his eyes brought Melanie off the bed. Together they searched the bedroom, then the living-room, but the medal wasn't in the apartment.

He ran into the bedroom struggled into his shirt, put on his holster, then his jacket.

Melanie said fearfully, "What is it, Johnny? Tell me!"

"Go to bed ... wait for me," and he left the apartment. He paused to search the corridor, then the cage of the elevator ... no medal. He rode down to the lobby, searched that, then went out onto the street. He was shaking now. He paused to drag down lungfuls of damp air as he tried to control his rising panic.

This was no way to act, he told himself. Where had he dropped the medal? Unlocking his car, he searched around the driver's seat ... no medal.

He relocked the car and stood thinking. It could have dropped anywhere, but if it had dropped in Andy's office, he was cooked. God! Was he cooked! All his plans, his confident two-year wait before he bought the boat would be shrivelled in the heat that Massino would turn on. Leaving his medal in Andy's office was like leaving a signed confession that he had taken the money!

There was still a chance. He started to his car, then stopped. Think straight, you fool! he told himself. It could still be all right. Leave the car ... it's part of your alibi!

He started down the street in a shambling run, covered the same ground, moving down the back streets, deserted but for a stray cat or an old drunk, sleeping in the doorway.

He had to make sure the medal wasn't in Andy's office. It didn't matter if it were found in the elevator, in Massino's office, but it would be fatal if it were found in Andy's office because no one except Andy and Benno were ever allowed into the office.

Breathing heavily, Johnny reached the corner of the street that led directly to Massino's office block. He came to an abrupt stop as he saw a police prowl car parked outside the office block.

Too late!

Benno had recovered and had alerted the fuzz and even as Johnny stood there in the shadows, he saw a Lincoln pull up and from it spilled Toni and Ernie who chased into the building.

Where had he dropped the medal?

As long as you wear it nothing really bad can happen to you.

He was no longer wearing it and he was superstitious enough to be certain that the medal was lying in front of the safe: a signed confession that he had taken the money! He looked across at the Greyhound station. He hadn't the nerve to go there, to take the two heavy bags and lug them back to his car. Toni or Ernie might look out of the window, down into the street and spot him. Anyway, now he dare not use his car. All the mob knew it by sight. He would have to go on the run. If he acted fast, he could make it. The money would be safe in the locker. He would wait until the heat cooled off, then sneak back, get the money and sneak out. He knew he was thinking like an idiot, but panic had its grip on him.

With screaming sirens, more police cars arrived. Then as Johnny stood against the wall, watching, his heart hammering, Massino's Rolls swept to the kerb. He watched Massino get out of his car and walk fast across the sidewalk and into the building.

He had to get out of town and fast, Johnny thought. Money? He must have money if he was to keep one jump ahead of Massino. He thought of all that money stashed away in the locker. No use to him right now. He had to have an immediate get-away stake.

Melanie? She never had any money. His mind raced. Maybe he was panicking for nothing. The medal could be anywhere, but in his bones, he was sure it was in Andy's office

Sammy!

Sammy had three thousand dollars under his bed. Johnny had to have money! He couldn't hide from Massino without money.

He began to run down the back streets. It was a long run. Sammy's pad was half way across the town. The City's clock was striking the half hour as Johnny, panting, started up the stairs that led to Sammy's fourth-floor pad. He knocked on Sammy's door, but there was no answer. He listened, knocked again, then turned the handle: the door swung open.

"Sammy?"

His fingers groped and found the light switch and snapped it down.

The tiny room held a truckle bed, a two-ringed gas cooker, an armchair, a battered TV set, but no Sammy. Then Johnny remembered Sammy always shacked up with his girl, Cloe, on Friday nights.

He moved into the room and shut the door. Kneeling, he groped under the bed and found a small steel box in which Sammy had told him he kept his savings. He pulled the box out. It wasn't even locked! Lifting the lid he saw the box was crammed with ten dollar bills. He didn't hesitate, acutely aware that every second he wasted decreased his chances of escape.

He stuffed his pockets with the bills, leaving the box empty. For a brief moment he wondered how Sammy would react, then he told himself he was only borrowing the money. In a short while, he would repay Sammy with interest.

Leaving the room, he started down the stairs. Now to get out of town! He wondered how long the fuzz would take to set up road blocks. Here was the danger, but he had to get out! His fingers touched the butt of his .38. If he had to, he would shoot his way out!

Moving into the street, his mind raced. He had to have a hideout! Somewhere where he could be completely lost for at least a month. Where could he go? Then he thought of Giovanni Fusseli. It was an inspired thought. Fusseli had been Johnny's father's best friend. He must be over seventy now. Maybe he was dead! Johnny had heard from him five years ago. He had been living in a small town – what the hell was it's name? Jackson? Packson? Jackson! It was on the freeway to Miami. If he could get there, he was sure Fusseli would shelter him.

He would have to steal a car. If he could get to Reddy's café where all the south-bound truckers stopped for a meal, he could bribe one of them to take him to Jackson.

He stood hesitatingly as he looked up and down the street. There were a number of cars parked. As he started towards them, he saw the headlights of a car swing into the street and he stepped back into the shadows. The car came slowly towards him, then pulled up by the kerb and immediately under a street light. A young, thin man with shoulder-length hair got out of the car. The street light showed Johnny his shabbiness: tattered jeans and a dirty sweat shirt. Acting on impulse and as the young man was locking the car door, Johnny stepped up to him.

"Want to earn twenty bucks?" Johnny asked quietly. The young man stared at him.

"Doing what?"

"Drive me to Reddy's café."

"Hey, man! That's twenty miles out of town!"

"At a dollar a mile, is that so rough?"

The young man grinned.

"You've got yourself a deal. Let's have the bread and we're on our way."

Johnny gave him a ten dollar bill.

"You get the rest when we get there."

"Fine ... I'm Joey. Who are you, buster?"

"Charlie," Johnny said. "Let's go." He waited until Joey had unlocked the car door, then got into the passenger's seat. Joey slid under the driving wheel.

"Listen, Joey, keep to the back streets. Drive fast, but not too fast ... get it?"

Joey laughed.

"Like that, huh? The fuzz bothering you?"

"You don't earn twenty bucks flapping with your mouth," Johnny said quietly. The cold menace in his voice made Joey stiffen. "Just drive."

At least, Johnny thought, this punk knows the City. Although it took longer, Joey kept to the back streets and in ten minutes or so they approached the freeway out of the City.

This was where trouble could be waiting, Johnny thought and he eased his gun in its holster for a quick draw. But there was no trouble. Johnny wasn't to know that road blocks were set up thirty minutes after he had left the City.

The Police Commissioner had been out of town and the Assistant Police Commissioner had no time for Massino. He was deliberately unco-operative, delaying the roadblocks, throwing his rank at Massino, pointing out that the Numbers gamble was illegal anyway.

Massino, raging, now regretted he hadn't taken care of the Assistant Police Commissioner as he had taken care of his boss with a new car every year, money to take care of his goddamn kids' education and a big insurance policy to take care of his goddamn wife.

Johnny paid Joey off, watched him drive away, then walked into Reddy's café to find a trucker who would drive him south.

His panic was slowly subsiding. So far ... so good.

Now for Jackson and a safe hide-away.

4

The shrilling of the telephone bell brought Joe Massino instantly awake. He snapped on the bedside lamp, looked at the clock that told him it was 03.15 and knew immediately that something had happened. No one would dare disturb his sleep unless there was an emergency.

He snatched up the receiver and swung his feet to the floor, stripping the blanket and sheet off his wife, Dina, who was coming awake with a low, moaning sound.

"Yeah?" Massino's voice boomed over the line.

"Boss ... this is Benno. The dough's gone. I've got a cracked nut. What do I do, boss?"

Massino knew Benno's limitations: he was a punch drunk, a goddamn moron, but at least he had got the message across. Massino felt a hot wave of murderous rage sweep through him, but he controlled it.

"Call the cop house, Benno," he said. "Get them with you. I'm on my way." He slammed down the receiver and began to strip off his pyjamas.

Dina, a blonde, heavily built woman, some fifteen years younger than her husband was now awake.

"What is it, for God's sake? What are you doing?"

"Shut up!" Massino snarled. He shoved his legs into his trousers and not bothering for a tie, he struggled into his jacket.

"That's a nice way to talk." She hauled up the blanket and sheet and covered herself. "Can't you act like a human?"

Massino left the bedroom, slamming the door after him. He hesitated for a moment, then going into his study he called Andy Lucas. He waited a long minute before Andy's voice came on the line.

"The money's been snatched." Massino told him. "Get over there ... get the boys," and he hung up.

Going down to the garage, he got into the Rolls and began the three mile haul across the City to his downtown office.

As he pulled up outside the office block, he saw a prowl car and Toni's Lincoln parked by the kerb. Well, at least he was getting some action, he thought as he rode up to the sixth floor in the elevator. There were two cops standing around looking vague. They stiffened to attention when they saw Massino. Both cops worked in Massino's district and were well looked after. They saluted as Massino stormed into Andy's office.

Benno was sitting on a chair, blood on his face, his eyes glazed. Toni stood by the window. Ernie stood by the open safe.

"What happened?" Massino demanded, coming to rest before Benno who made an effort to stand up but promptly sat down again.

"There was a fire, boss," he mumbled and his hand went to his head. "I opened up and there was a newspaper burning. While I was putting it out, I got clubbed."

"Who did it?" Massino barked.

"I dunno ... didn't see no one ... just got clubbed."

Massino went to the safe, looked inside, looked at the lock, then went to the telephone. He dialled a number while Ernie, Toni, Benno and the two cops watched him.

"I want Cullen," he said when a woman's sleepy voice answered. "This is Massino."

"Oh, Mr Massino!" The woman's voice came fully awake. "Jack is out of town. He's attending a conference in New York."

Massino cursed and slammed down the receiver. He took out an address book from his wallet, checked a number and dialled.

Assistant Police Commissioner Fred Zatski answered. He sounded outraged to be woken at this hour.

"Who the hell is this?"

"Massino. Listen, I want this goddamn town sewn up fast: road blocks, the railroad station, the bus station and the airport. I've had a $186,000 steal and the bastard will try to get out of town. Get moving! Hear me! Seal the whole goddamn town!"

"Just who do you imagine you're talking to?" Zatski bellowed. "Alert headquarters! Don't bother me! And listen, Massino, you may imagine you're someone in this town, but to me, you're just a bladder of wind," and he hung up.

Massino's face turned purple with rage. He yelled at the two cops, "Get moving, you hunkheads! Get someone who can do something here ... hear me!"

As O'Brien, the older of the two, jumped to the telephone, Andy Lucas came in. He had obviously come in a hurry. He was wearing a jacket and trousers over his pyjamas.

He looked into the safe, then at the lock, then met Massino's enraged eyes.

"It's an inside job," he said. "He'll try to run. He had a key."

"You telling me?" Massino snarled. "Think I'm blind! Cullen's out of town and this bastard Zatski won't play!"

O'Brien said, "Excuse me, Mr Massino, Lieutenant Mulligan with the squad is on his way."

Massino looked around the room like an enraged bull hunting for a target.

"Where's Johnny? I want my best man around me!"

"He didn't answer when I called him," Andy said. "He's not at home."

"I want him here!" Massino pointed at Toni. "Don't stand around like a goddamn dummy... get Johnny!"

As Toni left the office, Andy said quietly, "We'd better talk, Mr Joe."

Massino snorted. He nodded at Ernie.

"Get Benno to hospital," and leaving the office he crossed the passage, unlocked his office door and went in, followed by Andy.

He sat down at his desk and stared at Andy who sat on the corner of the desk.

"We're in trouble," Andy said. "At midday we have to pay out or there'll be a riot. We've got to borrow the money, Mr Joe, or we're sunk. If the newspapers get hold of this the Numbers will come under the limelight and Cullen will also be in trouble."

"So?"

"Tanza is our only chance. It'll cost, but we've got to go to him."

Massino clenched his big fists but he knew Andy was talking sense. The wail of a police siren sounded.

"You handle Mulligan," he said. "Get the town sealed off. I'll talk to Tanza."

"Whoever took the money is out of town by now," Andy said, "but we'll go through the motions." He went out, closing the door.

Massino pulled the telephone towards him, hesitated, then dialled a number. As he did so, he looked at his desk clock. The time now was 04.25.

Carlo Tanza was the headman of the Mafia cell in town. He was just one of the many arms of the Mafia octopus: a man of power, to whom Massino paid a weekly cut on his Numbers racket, his loan shark service and his vice earnings.

Tanza answered the telephone himself. He, like Massino, had come immediately awake, knowing no telephone bell would ring in his big, opulent house at this hour unless there was an emergency and Tanza's needle-sharp brain was always geared to meet an emergency.

He listened to what Massino had to say and produced a solution without hesitation.

"Okay, Joe. Don't worry about the money. By ten o'clock you'll have it for the payout. We'll keep the press out of this." A pause. "It'll cost you. Twenty-five per cent, but you've got to have it, so you've got to pay for it."

"Hey! Now wait!" Massino did sums in his head. This steal would cost him $46,000 out of his own pocket! "You can't screw me that hard. I'll pay fifteen."

"Twenty-five," Tanza said. "The money in your office at ten. You couldn't get it anywhere else. Now ... who did it?"

"All I know it was an inside job," Massino said. "It's just happened. I'll find out who did it, you can bet your life on that! I'm having the town sealed off, but the chances are the bastard's out by now."

"As soon as you know, tell me," Tanza said. "I'll turn the organization after him. Just let me know his name and we'll find him."

"Yeah. It must be one of my punks. Well, thanks, Carlo. I knew I could rely on you." A pause, "How about twenty per cent?"

Tanza chuckled.

"You're a trier, Joe. I have to work by rule. If it was me I'd let you have it for ten, but this will be New York money and it comes pricey," and he hung up.

Massino sat for a long moment, his face ugly with rage. Then, shoving back his chair, he strode out into the passage and into Andy's office.

Lieutenant Mulligan, a fat, freckled-faced man was examining the safe. Two other plain clothes detectives were finger printing. Benno and Ernie had gone. Andy stood just inside the doorway, nibbling his thumbnail.

"The road blocks are going up, Mr Massino," Mulligan said. "If he hasn't got away by now, he won't get away."

Knowing some thirty vital minutes had been wasted, Massino glared at the detective and then spat on the floor.

* * *

Toni Capello had been told to find Johnny. As he got into his Lincoln, he decided that the most likely place where Johnny would be found was with his girl friend, Melanie.

Toni envied Johnny. This lush, well built girl was his idea of a good lay. He thought it would be fun to batter on the door and get Johnny out of bed. Who knows? The girl might even come to the door herself.

He knew her name and where she lived. Once, he had spotted Johnny and the girl leave a restaurant and because he had the hots for her and nothing better to do, he had followed them back to Melanie's pad.

It took him only a few minutes to reach the street and he saw Johnny's car parked outside the apartment block. He grinned as he pulled up behind the car.

So Johnny was up there with his whore, Toni thought as he crossed the sidewalk. Man! Was he in for a shock!

He rode up in the elevator. Reaching Melanie's front door, he dug his fingers into the bell push and kept it there.

There was a long delay, then the door jerked open.

Melanie, holding a cotton wrap around her, stared at him, terror in her eyes.

"What is it?" she demanded, her voice strident.

What goes on? Toni wondered. This chick's flipping her lid.

"I want Johnny ... get him out of bed! The boss wants him pronto."

"He's not here!" Melanie began to shut the door, but Toni's foot came forward, blocking it.

"He is here, baby. Don't fool around. His car's outside. He's wanted." Then raising his voice, he yelled, "Hey, Johnny! The boss wants you!"

"I tell you he's not here!" Melanie cried. "Get out! He's not here!"

"Is that right?" Toni moved forward, pushing her back. "Then where is he?"

"I don't know!"

"His car's outside."

"I tell you I don't know!" She waved imploring hands to the door. "Go away ... get out!"

Suspicion lit a spark in Toni's mind. Why was she so frightened? Why was Johnny's car outside if he wasn't here?

Shoving her aside, he went into the bedroom and turned on the light. He looked around, then saw Johnny's tie on the floor.

"He's been here," he said as Melanie, shaking, came to the bedroom door. "Where did he go?"

"I don't know! I don't know anything! Get out!"

Jesus! Toni thought, it couldn't have been Johnny? Not Johnny! He caught hold of her wrist, swung her around and flung her down on the bed. He bent over her.

"Talk, baby, or I'll soften you. Where's he gone?"

Shuddering, Melanie tried to sit up. Toni placed his hand over her face and flung her back, then he repeated, "Where is he?"

"I don't know," Melanie sobbed.

He slapped her twice, jerking her head from side to side. "Where is he?" he yelled at her. "Come on, baby, spill it!"

She lay stunned by the force of the slaps.

"I don't know," she mumbled, trying to shield her face. "I don't know anything!"

Toni hesitated. He was almost sure she was lying, but to knock Johnny Bianda's girl about could be asking for real trouble if he was making a mistake.

If Johnny suddenly walked in and caught him with this chick, Johnny would kill him. Toni had no doubt about that.

"Get your clothes on," he said. "You and me are going for a ride. Come on!"

"I won't go with you! Get out!" Melanie screamed. Then sliding down the bed away from him, she was on her feet and out into the sitting-room before he could stop her.

Cursing, Toni rushed after her, caught her at the front door and dragged her back into the bedroom. He pulled his gun and shoved the barrel into her chest.

"Get dressed!" he snarled.

She looked with horror at the gun, then he had no more trouble with her.

Twenty minutes later, he led her into Massino's office.

"Something stinks here, boss," he said as Massino glared first at him and then at Melanie. "Maybe you can talk to her." He went on to tell Massino about Johnny's car, about Melanie's terror and no Johnny.

"What are you trying to tell me?" Massino snarled. "You telling me Johnny took the money?"

"I'm telling you nothing. She'll tell you."

Massino turned his bloodshot, enraged eyes on Melanie who shrivelled under his glare.

"Where's Johnny?"

She began to sob helplessly.

"I don't know. He went out on a job ... that's what he called it. Don't touch me! He told me I was to be his alibi. He lost his medal ..."

Massino drew a long slow breath.

"Sit down," he said. "Here, Toni, give her a chair." Then he began to question Melanie who talked, terrified by the staring bloodshed eyes and the fat, stone-hard face.

"Okay," Massino said finally. "Take her home, Toni," and getting up he went into Andy's office where Lieutenant Mulligan was about to leave. Massino drew him aside. "I want you to pick up Johnny Bianda," he said. "Turn every goddamn cop you've got on the job. Keep it quiet ... understand?"

Mulligan gaped at him.

"Bianda? You think he's behind this?"

Massino grinned like a wolf.

"I don't know, but if you can't find him in four or five hours, he could be. Drop everything ... get after Bianda!"

*   *   *

At 10.00, Carlo Tanza arrived in a Cadillac with three bodyguards. With a wide, oily smile he watched them dump two heavy suitcases on Massino's desk.

Tanza was a short, stocky Italian with a balding head, a big paunch, tiny, evil eyes and lips like red wire.

He shook hands with Massino, waved his men out of the office, nodded to Andy who stayed to count the money, then sat down.

"There's the money, Joe," he said. "You ask, you get. How's that for service?"

Massino nodded.

"Thanks."

"The boss talked to me on the phone," Tanza said. "He wasn't pleased. If you want to hold on to your Numbers, Joe, you have got to wake up your ideas. This safe ..."

"I'm getting a new one."

"I guessed you would. Now, who took the money?"

"Nothing certain yet," Massino said, "but it points to Johnny Bianda. He's gone missing."

"Bianda?" Tanza looked startled. "I got the idea he was your best man."

"Yeah." Massino's face turned red and his little eyes glittered, "but it points to him," and he went on to tell Tanza about Melanie, the alibi and the fact Johnny's car was still parked outside Melanie's pad.

"You're sure the girl knows nothing?"

"I'm sure. I scared the crap out of the bitch."

"So what are you going to do?"

Massino closed his big hands into fists.

"If he's skipped town, I want the organization to go after him. If he's still in town, I'll find him."

"He can buy himself a lot of protection with all that dough," Tanza said thoughtfully. "Okay, I'll tell the Big Man. So you want us to find him ... right?"

"If he's not holed up here ... yes."

"I don't want to start something too soon, Joe. Once the organization gets moving it's hard to stop and it costs. Suppose you make certain he isn't in town, then give me the green light, huh?"

"If he's skipped, the longer you wait the further he'll go."

Tanza grinned evilly.

"It don't matter how far he goes ... if he goes to China, we'll find him. We've never failed yet. You make sure first he isn't in town, then we'll take over." He got to his feet. "I'm only trying to save you money, Joe. We don't work for nothing."

When Tanza had gone, Massino called Toni and Ernie into the office.

"Go to Johnny's place and search it." he ordered. "I want every scrap of information, every scrap of paper you can find there. I want you to send out some of the boys to ask around. I want to know who his friends are."

When they had left, Massino called Lieutenant Mulligan.

"Anything new?" he asked when the Lieutenant came on the line.

"It's my bet he's skipped town," Mulligan said. "There's no trace of him. I've dug up his record, his prison photo and his fingerprints. Would they be of any use to you?"

"Yeah. I want everything you've got on him."

"I'll send a man over with the photostats right away, Mr Massino."

"Would you know if he has any relatives?"

"Doesn't seem to from his record. His father died five years ago."

"Anything on him?"

"An Italian: worked in a fruit cannery in Tampa. Johnny was born there."

Massino thought for a moment.

"A dog to its vomit. He could be heading back South."

"Yeah. Do you want me to alert the Florida police ... can do."

Massino hesitated, then said, "No. I can handle this, but keep hunting for him in town." A pause, then Massino said, "The next time you're passing look in and see Andy. He'll have something for you."

As Mulligan began mumbling thanks, Massino hung up.

*　　*　　*

At 19.00, Massino was still at his desk. Spread out before him were the various items that Mulligan had sent him and that Toni and Ernie had found in Johnny's apartment.

Andy hovered behind him, chain smoking, but quiet. He could feel the intensity of Massino's vicious fury that was only just under control.

"So what have we got?" Massino demanded suddenly.

"He's our man," Andy said. "No question about it now and he's skipped town."

"Who the hell would have thought Johnny would have done this to me?" Massino asked, pushing back his chair. "The sonofabitch! Well, okay, I'll turn the organization after him. It may take time, but they'll find him and then he'll wish he'd never been born!"

Andy came to the desk.

"This interests me, Mr Joe," he said and picked up a much thumbed copy of *Yachts & Motorboats*, a technical magazine for boat builders that Toni had found in Johnny's apartment. "Why should Johnny have this?"

"How the hell should I know?" Massino snarled. "It means nothing!"

Andy was flicking through the pages, then he paused at an advert of a thirty-foot cabin cruiser that had been ringed by a pencil.

"Look at this."

Massino glared at him.

"So what?"

"Do you think Johnny is interested in boats? Do you think his plan was to skip in a boat?"

Massino became attentive.

"Yeah ... another pointer to the South."

"And this." Andy picked up a gaudy Christmas card that Toni had also found. Written in a spidery handwriting was the legend:

> *See you sometime.*
> *Giovanni Fuselli.*
> *Jackson.*

"Where the hell is Jackson and what's so important about this goddamn thing?"

"Jackson is around thirty miles from Jacksonville, Florida."

Then the telephone bell rang. Ernie was on the line. "Got something, boss," he said, his voice excited. "Just been talking to a young punk who says he gave a ride to a guy who matches up with Bianda's description. He dropped him off at Reddy's café."

"Get him over here. I'll show him Bianda's photo." Massino hung up, then looked at Andy. "Looks like Johnny got a ride out of town to Reddy's café: that's where the truckers stop before driving South, isn't it?"

"That's right."

"South!" Massino said. "It all points south, doesn't it? That's where the bastard's gone!"

Fifteen minutes later, Ernie, accompanied by Joey, looking uneasy, came into the office.

Massino pushed the photo across the desk.

"That him?"

Joey peered at the photo, then nodded.

"Yes, sir."

"Okay." Massino took out his wallet, found a five dollar bill and tossed it at Joey. "Get his name and address," he said to Ernie, "and get him out of here."

"Wait." Andy came forward as Joey started for the door. "This guy you gave a ride to was carrying two heavy bags ... right?"

Joey shook his head.

"He wasn't carrying a thing."

"He didn't have even one bag?"

"Nothing."

"Goddamn it!" Massino snarled. "He must have been carrying two bags!"

Joey paled, but shook his head.

"Honest, sir, he wasn't carrying a thing!"

"Okay," Andy said quietly, "take him away."

As the office door shut, Massino glared at Andy.

"You reckon the money's still in town?"

"No. Let's look at this, Mr Joe. Don't let's rush it."

Andy began to pace up and down and because Massino knew this little man was no fool, he restrained his impatience while he waited. Andy paused. "Bianda is a loner. He has no friends we've been able to dig up, yet he

72

gets this Christmas card so he does have someone. He takes off, but he hasn't the money with him and he must know he could never dare show his snout again in this town if he stashed it so it looks to me that he wasn't working alone. Call this a hunch, Mr Joe," Andy paused, then went on, "Suppose this other guy Bianda was working with rushed the money out of town while Bianda was looking for his medal? Are you getting my thinking, Mr Joe? Bianda and this other guy do the job. This other guy takes the money. Bianda goes back to his whore. The idea is none of us would suspect him of the steal. Then he finds the medal gone. He knows he's cooked if the medal is found in my office. He has to be sure, but Benno has the cops here so Bianda panics, gets a ride out of town and heads south to join this other guy." Andy leaned forward and tapped the Christmas card. "Fuselli. It's my guess he's this other guy."

Massino glowered at him.

"You're nuts! This Fuselli ... how do you know because he sent a Christmas card that he is working with Bianda?"

"I don't know, but Bianda is a loner and here is someone who kept in touch with him ... someone living south."

Massino hesitated.

"Well ... could be. I'll call Carlo. He'll turn the Florida mob onto Fuselli."

"Just a moment, Mr Joe," Andy said. "There's no rush to call in Tanza. We could handle this ourselves. Have you thought how much the Big Man will take if they go after Bianda? They would take half: $93,000! They could even take more. We know the way the Big Man operates. If he puts a finger on a man, sooner or later, that man's dead. It might take a couple of years, but once the sign is on, that man's dead. Suppose we send Toni and Ernie down to Jackson and check this Fuselli out first? If he's our man, we save ourselves $93,000. If he's in the clear and Bianda isn't there, then we turn it over to Tanza. We lose a few days, but we can afford to do that. What do you think?"

Massino considered this, then nodded.

"Now you're using your head, Andy," he said. "Okay, get those two off by the first plane. Let's take a look at Fuselli."

* * *

Ernie and Toni arrived at Jacksonville airport some minutes after 11.00. They went immediately to Hertz Rent-a-car bureau and hired a Chevvy. While waiting for the car, Ernie asked the girl the best way to Jackson.

"Follow the freeway to your right," he was told. "No problem: Jackson is signposted: around thirty miles from here."

Ernie got in the passenger's seat. When he could avoid any form of work, he did so. After all, Toni was five years his junior, was his reasoning, so why the hell shouldn't he do the driving?

On the freeway, he said, "Let's get this organized, Toni. If we run into Johnny, you take care of him and I'll take care of Fuselli ... right?"

Toni stiffened.

"Where do you get this I take care of Johnny crap?"

Ernie hid a sly grin.

"That's what you want, isn't it? You've always said you could beat Johnny to a draw. Looks to me, we're heading for a showdown. This is your chance to prove you're better and faster with a gun than he is."

Toni shifted uneasily. Johnny's past reputation had always hung over him like a dark cloud and was still hanging over him.

"Maybe both of us had better take care of him," he said. "That punk can shoot."

"So can you." Ernie relaxed. "Didn't you tell me only last week that Johnny was old and washed up? You take care of him. This Fuselli might be as fast as Johnny."

Toni felt sweat beads suddenly on his forehead.

"So that's fixed, huh?" Ernie said, enjoying himself. "We shoot first and talk after, huh?"

Toni didn't say anything. He was aware of a tight ball of fear in his guts. He drove in silence for ten miles, then aware that Ernie was dozing off, he said. "Do you think Johnny really took all that bread?"

"Why not?" Ernie shook himself awake and lit a cigarette. "Boy! Could I use money like that! You know something, Toni? Johnny has more guts than you or me."

"Maybe, but he can't get away with it. If we don't find him, the Big Man will. The bastard's stupid."

"Maybe, but he's tried and that's more than you and me would have done. There's always a chance he just might get away with it."

Toni glanced at his fat companion.

"You're nuts! No one has ever beaten the organization and no one ever will. If it takes years, they'll find him, if we don't."

"But think of what he could do with all that bread even if he lasted only two years."

"To hell with the money! I'd rather stay alive!"

"There's the signpost," Ernie said. "Jackson five miles."

"I can read," Toni said and the knot of fear in his guts tightened.

Jackson turned out to be a tiny fruit-growing town with a Main street, a number of fruit-canning factories and outlying farms.

Toni drove down the Main street, passing a small, clean looking hotel, the Post Office, a general store, a movie house and a café.

"What a goddamn hole," he said as he pulled up outside the café. "Let's have a beer. Maybe we can get a lead on Fuselli."

They were aware that the people on the street, mostly old women and older men were staring curiously at them. They went into the café, crossed to the bar and hoisted themselves up on stools.

There were a few old men sitting at tables, nursing glasses of beer, who gaped at them as if they were something out of a zoo.

The barman, fat, balding, with a friendly red face, came to them.

"Mornin' gents. What's your pleasure?"

"Beers," Ernie said.

"Nice to see strangers in our town," the barman went on as he drew beers, "Harry Dukes is the name. Welcome, gents."

In spite of his friendliness, Ernie could see Dukes was looking at them curiously as if trying to decide who and what they were. Toni's black-and-pink-flowered kipper tie seemed to be bothering him.

They drank, then Ernie said, "Nice little town you have here."

He always did the talking while Toni watched, listened and kept his mouth shut.

"Not so bad, and thank you. A bit quiet, but it could be worse. Lots of old people here, but in the evenings it livens up when the boys and girls come in from picking."

"Yeah." Ernie took out his wallet with a flourish and extracted a card he always carried around with him. The times this card had got him out of trouble and got him information were without number. He pushed the card across the counter.

"This for me?" Dukes asked startled.

"Just take a gander, friend."

Duke went to the back of his bar and found a pair of spectacles. He put them on while Toni hissed softly under his breath. Ernie nudged him and Toni subsided.

Dukes read:

THE ALERT DETECTIVE AGENCY
SAN FRANCISCO

Presented by: Detective 1st Grade Jack Loosey

He looked up, removed his spectacles and gaped. "This you?" he asked, tapping the card.

"Yeah, and this is my assistant: Detective Morgan," Ernie said.

Dukes whistled softly. He was obviously impressed.

"You know something? I had an idea there was something special about you two gents," he said. "Detectives, huh?"

"Private," Ernie said gravely. "Maybe you can help us."

Dukes took a step back. He began to look worried.

"Nothing in this little town for you, gents. I assure you."

"Have a drink and give us another beer."

Dukes hesitated, then drew three beers and stood, waiting.

"We get all kinds of jobs," Ernie said. "You've no idea. Does the name Giovanni Fuselli mean anything to you?"

"Sure does." Then Dukes stiffened and his eyes turned hostile. "What's he to you?"

Ernie grinned slyly.

"Nothing to me, Mr Dukes, but plenty to him. Does he live here?"

Dukes had now turned very hostile.

"If you want to know anything about Mr Fuselli you go to the cops," he said. "Mr Fuselli is a fine gentleman. You go to the cops: don't come here asking me questions."

Ernie sipped his beer and then laughed.

"You've got me all wrong, Mr Dukes. Our job is to find Mr Fuselli. We've been told what a fine man he is. We're trying to help him. Between you and me, a relative of his has left him some money: his aunt died last year and we're trying to clear up her estate."

Dukes' hostility went away like a fist opening into a hand. "Is that right? Mr Fuselli has come into money?"

"He sure has. It's not my business to tell you how much," Ernie winked confidently, "but it's a nice slice. We've been told he lives around here, but we haven't his address. Like I said: we get all kinds of jobs. This is one of the nice ones."

Listening, Toni marvelled at Ernie's glib talk and envied him. He knew he could never talk as convincingly as this.

"Well, I'm glad. Mr Fuselli is a good friend of mine," Dukes said. "Right now, he's away. What a shame! Left last week for a trip up north."

Ernie slopped some of his beer.

"Is that right? Do you know how long he'll be away?"

"No, sir. Mr Fuselli goes north from time to time. Sometimes he comes back in a week ... sometimes in a month, but he always comes back." Dukes grinned. "Just shuts up his little house and takes off."

"North? Where?"

Dukes shook his head.

"Mr Fuselli never says. He'll come in here, have a beer, then he says to me, 'Well, Harry, I guess I'll go north for a while. See you when I get back.' Mr Fuselli never talks about himself and I don't ask questions."

Ernie lit a cigarette while he thought.

"Doesn't someone look after his place while he's away?"

Dukes laughed.

"Not much of a place to look after. No, I guess no one goes near it. It's in a pretty lonely spot."

"Just where is it?"

"Out on Hampton's Hill. You being a stranger here wouldn't know Hampton's Hill, would you?"

Containing his impatience with an effort, Ernie agreed.

"Well, you go down Main street, take the dirt road to your left, drive up the hill for a couple of miles and pass Noddy Jenkin's farm. Then you go on for another mile and you'll see Mr Fuselli's place on your right: a little clapboard house, but he keeps it nice."

"We'd better write to him," Ernie said and finished his beer. "The address is Hampton Hill, Jackson?"

"Yeah. This is good news about him inheriting money. An aunt? Jesus! She must have been old. Mr Fuselli is pushing seventy."

Ernie gaped at him.

"Seventy?"

"That's right. He had his seventy-second birthday last month, but he's tough. Make no mistake about that ... spry as a man half his age."

"Well, I guess we'll be getting along. Nice meeting you, Mr Dukes."

After shaking hands, Ernie followed Toni out into the sunshine. "Canned stuff and bread and a bottle of Scotch."

"What the hell for?" Toni demanded.

"Go get enough food to last us a couple of days," Ernie said. "Can't you see all these old creeps are watching us?"

Toni went down the street to the general store while Ernie got into the passenger's seat of the car. He pushed his hat over his eyes and rested.

After a while Toni came back with a big bag of groceries and a bottle of Scotch. He put the bag on the back seat, then got under the driving wheel.

"So now what?"

"We go to Hampton Hill or whatever the hell it's called," Ernie said.

"Is that such a hot idea?"

"Use your nut. We flew down here. Johnny and Fuselli are driving down. We have four or five hours' start ahead of them. It's my bet they'll bring the money here. When they arrive, we'll be all over them before they know what's hit them, but we could have a wait."

Toni thought about this, then grunted.

"Okay."

Engaging gear, he drove fast along the broad road, lined on either side with trees heavy with oranges and headed for Hampton Hill.

5

A cup of coffee before him, Johnny sat at a small table and looked around the crowded café. There was a steady roar of voices as long-haul truckers greeted each other, ate hamburgers, swigged numerous cups of coffee, then heaved themselves to their feet and went out into the pale sunshine as other truckers came in.

Johnny glanced at his watch. The time was 05.25. He had to get moving soon, he told himself, but up to now, he had held back as every trucker seemed to know every other trucker and he was uneasy about approaching a group of them. He had tried one man who stood near him while waiting for ham and eggs, but the man shook his head.

"No luck, pal. No passengers: against the Company's rules."

Then a powerfully built man came in and Johnny noted with surprise no one greeted him. This man went to the bar and ordered pancakes and syrup and coffee, then looked around for a vacant seat.

Johnny waved to him and carrying the plate of food, the big man came over and sat down.

Johnny looked searchingly at him: an ex-boxer, he thought. The flat nose and the scar tissues made this an easy guess. The face was lined, worried and sullen and yet there was something likeable about this man.

"Hi!" the man said as he set down the food. "Joe Davis. This goddamn place is always over full."

"Al Bianco," Johnny said.

Davis began to eat while Johnny lit a cigarette. Again he looked at his watch. Time was moving along. He wondered if Massino had alerted the organization or what he was doing.

"Going south?" he asked.

Davis glanced up.

"Yeah. You ain't trucking?"

"Looking for a ride," Johnny said. "I pay my way. Would you be going near Jacksonville?"

"Right through to Vero Beach." Davis regarded Johnny, ate some more, then said, "You're welcome. It won't cost you a thing. I welcome company."

"Thanks." Johnny finished his coffee. "You reckon to take off soon?"

"As soon as I've got this junk down my throat. It's a hell of a haul."

"I'll be outside, waiting." Johnny said and got to his feet. "I'll get myself a wash."

After paying for his coffee, Johnny went into the toilet, washed his face and hands, then went out into the cool crisp air.

He stood around, watching the big trucks take off and go roaring down the freeway. What a hell of a job! he thought. Then his mind again switched to Massino. He felt a little knot of fear. He knew the organization had never failed to find their man, nor failed to kill him.

There is always the first time, he told himself and grinned mirthlessly. Who knows? He could make history. The first man to beat the Mafia. With the cold wind fanning his face, he felt confident. Who knows?

Davis came out of the café and Johnny joined him. They went across to an old, beaten-up truck full of empty orange crates.

"Here she is," Davis said. "A real bitch! I've one more haul, then I get a new one if I'm lucky. Man! Has this old cow done some mileage!"

He swung himself up into the cab. Johnny went around and got into the passenger's seat. The cab stank of sweat, oil and gas fumes. The springs of his seat dug into his buttocks. This was going to be one hell of a ride he thought.

Davis started the motor. As it came to life, there was a grinding noise as if something had come apart in the engine.

"Don't worry about the noise," Davis said, "She's still got enough guts to get us south." He rammed in the gear, then drove on to the freeway.

Johnny felt the vibration of the protesting motor shake him from head to foot. The roar of the motor made conversation impossible. He braced himself, thinking of the miles ahead, but at least now he was moving into safety.

"An old cow, huh?" Davis shouted and grinned at Johnny.

Johnny nodded.

The two men sat silent as the tyres ate up the miles. Trucks and cars roared by them. With sixty miles on the clock, the engine note suddenly changed and the din quietened.

Davis looked at Johnny and grinned.

"It takes this far for her to start to behave," he said. Johnny could now hear him easily. "She hates work, but when she does work, she ain't all that bad."

Then he did something that shocked Johnny. He clenched his fist and slammed it against his forehead. He did this three times: powerful blows that would have stunned most men.

"Hey! For God's sake! You'll hurt yourself!" Johnny exclaimed.

Davis grinned.

"Anything is better than the way my head aches. Had this bitch of a headache for months. A couple of bangs sets it right. Forget it, Al, as I forget it."

"You suffer from headaches?" Johnny asked.

"Oh, sure. If you had been in my game, you'd have headaches too." Davis increased the speed of the truck.

Believe it or not, one time I was heavyweight contender for the crown." He grinned. "Never made it, but I was sparring partner for Ali at his greatest. Man! Did I have a ball!" He snorted. "All gone now. All I've got is a nagging wife and this old truck."

Johnny suddenly realized there was something badly wrong with this man: something that made him uneasy. He remembered all the truckers in Reddy's café hadn't spoken to Davis nor even waved to him.

"Your head ache now?" he asked.

"It's fine. I give the old nut three or four wams and then it behaves itself."

Johnny lit a cigarette. "Want a smoke?"

"Not me. Never have, never will. Where are you from, Al?"

"New York," Johnny lied. "I've never been south ... thought I'd take a look."

"Sort of travelling light, huh?"

"My stuff's coming by train."

"Good idea." A long pause, then Davis said, "Did you see Cooper knock Ali on his pants?"

"Saw it on the telly."

"I was right there. You ever been in London?"

"No."

"Ali took me with the rest of the mob. Some city." Davis grinned. "Those chicks! Skirts way up beyond their fannies." He thumped his head again. "You see Frazier beat Ali?"

"On the telly."

"I was right there. He'll come back ... the greatest."

Johnny stared through the dusty windshield. They were driving between citrus orchards, either side of the freeway. He looked at his watch. The time was now 07.30.

"How long to Jacksonville?"

"Ten hours if this bitch keeps going. You in a hurry?"

"I've all the time in the world."

There was a long silence as the truck roared on, then Davis asked, "You married?"

"Me? No."

"I guessed that. You wouldn't be on a trip like this if you were. You know something? A guy can find a good woman or a bad woman ... I guess I had no luck."

Johnny didn't say anything.

"You're lucky not to have kids," Davis went on. "I've got a girl. Sex is all she thinks about and her mother doesn't give a goddamn." Davis thumped his head so violently Johnny winced. "What can you do? If I took a strap to her, the cops would arrive. There ain't a thing a father can do if his daughter has the hots."

Johnny thought of Melanie. What was happening to her? Had Massino ...? He flinched and forced the thought from his mind.

"Getting hot." Davis said and wiped his face with the back of his hand. "This is a hell of a haul." He kept the shuddering truck at seventy miles an hour. They were now out of the farming country and coming to the swampland. "This I hate," Davis said. "Snakes, jungle ... you watch it. We'll get by. After a while, we'll come to the real country ... the south!"

Watching this big man as he crouched over the driving wheel, seeing the glazed expression in his eyes, Johnny knew something bad was about to happen.

"You're driving too fast!" he shouted. "Cut it down!"

"You call this fast?" Davis turned his head to look at Johnny who felt a chill go up his spine. The small eyes with their scar tissue were turning sightless. "The greatest ... like me! He'll come back!"

"Watch the road!" Johnny shouted. "Joe!"

Davis grinned stupidly, then took his hands off the steering wheel and began to beat his head. Johnny made a grab at the wheel but he was too late. The truck roared off the freeway and with screaming tyres, it ploughed into the jungle.

Thrown against the cabin door, Johnny felt the door give and felt himself falling. He landed on his back in a thick flowering bush that broke his fall, then he rolled to the ground.

He lay stunned, listening to the truck ploughing through the thicket, then came the sound of a grinding crash as the truck hit a tree. As he struggled upright, the gas tank of the truck exploded and the truck went up in a roaring sheet of flame.

Johnny started towards the blaze, then saw it was hopeless. His sense of self-preservation asserted itself. Within minutes a prowl car would arrive. It would be fatal if the cops found him. They would question him, search him, and the moment they found he had a gun and three hundred ten dollar bills stuffed into his pockets, he would be cooked.

He started down a narrow path that led into the jungle, aware that his right ankle hurt. He forced himself along, limping now and frightened that he had suffered an injury that might develop into something bad.

He hadn't gone more than five hundred yards when he heard the wail of a siren. He broke into a limping run, stumbled and fell flat.

Hell! he thought. I've hurt my goddamn self! He scrambled to his feet and set off again, but this time he was in bad pain and was dragging his leg. After a hundred yards or so, with cold sweat running down his face, he could go no further. He looked around. To his right was a big clump of tangled undergrowth. He forced his way to it, then collapsed on the damp ground. Sure that anyone coming down the path couldn't see him, he stretched out his aching leg and prepared to wait.

* * *

What Johnny couldn't know was that this accident had saved his life. Had Davis delivered him to Jacksonville, Johnny would have walked into the trap Ernie and Toni had set up.

He didn't know, and he cursed his luck as he lay in the undergrowth feeling his leg slowly stiffening. He had been lying there for the past four hours.

The police, the ambulance and the breakdown truck had come and gone. The jungle was cool, and Johnny, badly shaken, was content to lie there and wait. He suffered. His ankle was swelling and when he looked at it, he saw with alarm it looked red and angry. Had he broken it? Maybe it was just a bad sprain. The thoughts of putting his weight on it made him flinch.

Later, he became thirsty. He looked at his watch. The time was now 13.05. He would have to make an effort to get to the freeway. With any luck he would pick up a ride. He had to get to Jackson!

He crawled out of the thicket and on to the path. He could smell the burned-out truck and the undergrowth that had gone up with it. On the path, he forced himself up on one leg, then gently he put a little of his weight on his damaged ankle. Pain raved up from the ankle into his head.

Jesus! he thought. I'm in goddamn trouble! He sank down, feeling sweat break out on his face and a light feeling of faintness that frightened him.

He had better wait, he thought. He had better get back into the undergrowth. Maybe later, he would be able to use his leg.

He began to crawl back towards the undergrowth when he saw the snake.

The thick-bodied Cottonmouth was coiled within eight feet of him. It raised its olive green head and its forked tongue darted.

Johnny turned cold, the pain in his ankle forgotten. He had a horror of snakes. He lay there, motionless, not even blinking, watching the snake. Apart from its darting tongue, it too remained motionless.

Minutes dragged by. Johnny thought of his gun. Should he try to shoot the snake? Then he thought of the danger. Someone might hear the sound of the shot and come to investigate. Maybe the snake would go away if he waited long enough. Would it attack him? It could be harmless. He had no knowledge of snakes and wasn't to know that a Cottonmouth was lethal.

Then slowly the snake began to uncoil while Johnny watched it with horror. The snake slid into the undergrowth where Johnny had been hiding. With the back of his hand, Johnny wiped away the sweat streaming down his face. Had that green nightmare been in the thicket with him?

He had to get out of here!

The sun was now penetrating the over-hanging trees. What wouldn't he have given for a drink? The jungle could be swarming with snakes! Again he hoisted himself on one leg. He began hopping down the path towards the freeway. He had only taken four hops when he lost balance. The whole weight of his body came down on his injured ankle. He heard himself cry out as pain raved through him, then he fell, his head thumping down on a tree root and blackness swept over him.

*　　*　　*

"If they're coming they should have been here by now," Ernie said. He had just finished a can of pork and beans and he released a gentle belch.

He and Toni were sitting in a ditch that gave them a direct view of the small clapboard house where Fuselli lived. Their car was out of sight behind a clump of trees, a quarter of a mile further down the dirt road.

"So okay ... so what?" Toni was slightly drunk. To bolster up his nerve, he had been hitting the bottle.

"I'm going into town to call the boss." Ernie said. "He'll be wondering what we're doing. We've been sitting in this goddamn ditch for eight hours."

"So what?" Toni repeated. "They could have had a blow-out. You stick here, Ernie. Don't get your bowels in an uproar." He reached for a can of stewed steak. "They could show any minute."

Ernie got to his feet.

"I'm going. You stay here."

"The hell with that!" Toni wasn't too drunk to realize that on his own if Johnny showed up, he could be in trouble. "You stick right here! Let's give them a couple of hours, then we both go down town."

"Shut up!" Ernie snarled. "You stick here." Climbing out of the ditch. He walked down the road to where the car was hidden.

Twenty minutes later, he was talking to Massino. He explained the situation.

"Right now, boss, we're staked out, out of sight, in front of Fuselli's pad, but it's eight hours now. They should have been here four hours back. Toni reckons they could have had a blow out or something. I don't know. What do I do?"

"Could be Toni's right," Massino said. "Stick around, Ernie, if they don't show by eight o'clock tomorrow, come on back."

"Anything you say, boss," Ernie said, thinking of the discomfort of spending a night in the ditch.

Massino slammed down the receiver, then turned to Andy who was prowling around the office. He told him what Ernie had said.

"There's one thing we should have done, Mr Joe," Andy said. "We should have checked out Reddy's café. I'll do it. We should have thought of that right away."

"I want you here!" Massino snapped. "Get someone to do it! Send Lu Berilli!"

"I'll do it myself," Andy said firmly. He was sick of staying in the office listening to Massino cursing Johnny.

"I'll ..." Then he stopped as he saw Massino glaring at him, his little eyes like red, flaming buttons.

"You stay here!" Massino snarled. "Don't forget you're the only punk who had the key to the safe? So, you stay here until I find Johnny and the money!"

Andy was expecting this.

"And if you don't find him?"

"Then I'll start looking at you! Tell Berilli to go to the café and ask around."

"You're the boss, Mr Joe," Andy said and reaching for the telephone he instructed Lu Berilli to go to Reddy's café.

Three hours later, Lu Berilli came hurriedly into Massino's office. Berilli was a tall, thin Italian, around thirty years of age with a movie-star profile and a success with women. Massino considered him a bright boy and he was right. Berilli had a good brain, but Massino knew his limitations. There was a yellow streak in Berilli: he had no stomach for violence, and that meant he couldn't rise very high in Massino's kingdom.

"You've taken your goddamn time!" Massino snarled.

"I wanted to get this dead right, Mr Joe," Berilli said quietly. "And I've got it right." He produced a one inch to the mile map and spread it on Massino's desk. Leaning forward, he tapped with a manicured fingernail. "Right here, Mr Joe, is where I guess Bianda is at this moment."

Massino, surprised, stared at the map, then up at Berilli.

"What the hell are you talking about?"

"From my information, Johnny got a ride with a punchdrunk trucker," Berilli said. "Heading south. I was told this trucker was due to blow his top. That's what he did. The truck went off the freeway around seventy miles an hour just here." Berilli again tapped the map. "The trucker was killed. There was a hell of a smash. There's no trace of

Bianda, but he has to be hurt. If we act fast, it's my bet he's holed up somewhere in this bit of jungle I've marked. If we get the mob down there pronto, we could flush him out."

Massino's lips came off his teeth in a snarling grin.

"Good work, Lu," he said, then raising his voice, he bawled for Andy.

*　　*　　*

Johnny felt cold water on his face that trickled into his mouth. He became aware of a shadowy figure bending over him. Fear clutched at him and he struggled up, shaking his head, forcing his eyes into focus. Then the figure bending over him became clear: a thin, bearded man, wearing a bush hat and khaki drill. He had a hooked nose and the sharpest, clearest blue eyes Johnny had ever seen.

"Take it easy," the man said gently. "You've found a friend."

Johnny struggled up into a sitting position. He was immediately aware of a dull, throbbing pain in his head and a sharp, grinding pain in his right ankle.

"I've bust my ankle," he said, then grabbed hold of the water bottle the man was holding and drank thirstily. "Phew!" He lowered the bottle and regarded the man suspiciously.

"You have a bad sprain," the man said. "No bones broken. Just take it easy. I'll get an ambulance. Do you live around here?"

"Who are you?" Johnny asked. His hand slid inside his coat and his sweating fingers closed around the butt of his gun.

"I'm Jay Freeman," the man said and smiled. He was squatting on his heels. "You take it easy. I'll get you fixed."

"No!"

The snap in Johnny's voice made Freeman look sharply at him.

"Are you in trouble, friend?" he asked.

Friend?

No one had ever used that word to him. Friend?

It was now Johnny's turn to look sharply at Freeman and what he saw was reassuring.

"You call it that," he said. "I'm in a spot, but I've got money. Can you put me under the wraps until this goddamn ankle is okay?"

Freeman patted Johnny's sweat-soaked arm.

"I told you ... take it easy. Is it police trouble?"

"More than that."

"Put your arm around my neck. Let's go."

With surprising strength, he got Johnny up on his left foot, then, supporting him, he helped him hop along the path until they reached the edge of the jungle where an old, broken-down Ford stood, parked in the shade.

Johnny was sweating and in pain as Freeman helped him into the car.

"Relax," Freeman said as he slid under the driving wheel. "You've nothing to worry about."

Johnny relaxed. The pain in his ankle kept him from talking. He just lay against the worn plastic seat, thankful he was moving.

He was dimly aware of being driven along the freeway, then up a dirt road, then along a narrow path where tree branches scraped against the sides of the car.

"Here's home," Freeman said and brought the car to a stop.

Johnny raised his head. He stared at a low-built log cabin, set in a clearing with trees overshadowing it. It looked good and safe to him.

"No problem," Freeman said as he got out of the car. "You can rest up here."

He half carried, half dragged Johnny into the cabin that consisted of a living-room, two bedrooms and a shower room. It was sparsely furnished and one side of the living-room was lined with books.

Freeman got Johnny into the smaller bedroom and propped him up against the wall. Then he stripped off the cotton coverlet on the bed and with care, steered him around and got him onto the bed.

"Just relax," Freeman said and went away.

Johnny's ankle hurt so badly, he only half registered what was going on. He lay on the bed, staring up at the wooden ceiling, not believing this was happening to him.

Freeman returned with a glass of ice cold beer in his hand. "Drink this." He gave Johnny the beer. "I'll look at your ankle."

Johnny drank the beer in one gorgeous gulp. He set the glass down on the floor.

"Thanks! Man! Did I need that!"

"It's a bad sprain," Freeman told him. He had got Johnny's shoe and sock off. "It can be fixed. In a week, you'll be able to walk."

Johnny half sat up.

"A week?"

"You're safe here, friend," Freeman said, "No one ever comes here. Maybe you're a stranger in this district. I'm known as the Snake Man, and you have no idea the horror people have of snakes."

Johnny stared at him.

"Snakes?"

"I catch snakes. It's a living. I work with the hospitals. They're always yelling for serum: I supply them. Right now I have three hundred venomous snakes in cages behind this cabin. People keep clear of me." While he was talking, he bound Johnny's ankle with a bandage soaked in iced water. Already the pain was lessening. "Feel like eating? I've been out all morning and I haven't had a bite. Want to join me?"

"I could eat a horse," Johnny said.

Freeman chuckled.

"That's something not on the menu," he said. "Won't be long."

Within ten minutes he came back with two soup plates full of thick, savoury-smelling stew. He sat on the end of the bed, handed Johnny one of the plates and began to eat. When Johnny had finished, he decided it was about the best meal he had eaten in years.

"You're some cook!" he said. "Never tasted anything so good."

"Yes ... rattlesnake meat when cooked the right way, is pretty good," Freeman said, collecting the plates.

Johnny's eyes opened wide.

"That snake meat?"

"I live on it."

"Well, for God's sake!"

Freeman laughed.

"A lot better than horse." He went away and Johnny heard him washing up.

After a while, Freeman came back into the small bedroom.

"I've things to do," he said. "You don't have to worry. No one comes here. I'll be back in three or four hours." He eyed the beginning of a beard on Johnny's face. "Want to shave? I have a cordless."

Johnny shook his head.

"I reckon on growing a beard."

The two men looked at each other, then Freeman nodded.

"Take a nap. I'll lock you in," and he went away.

Although his head and his ankle still ached, Johnny slid into sleep. When he awoke the light was fading and he felt a lot better. His headache had gone away, but his ankle still bothered him.

Lying there, looking out of the window, watching the sun sink behind the trees, he wondered about Freeman. An oddball, he told himself, but someone he felt he could trust. Instinctively, he was sure of that.

He turned his thoughts to Massino. Having worked so long for him, Johnny could guess how he was reacting: like an enraged bull.

How long would it be before he went to Tanza and asked the organization to take over? Maybe the organization was already hunting for him. Johnny thought of all that money stashed away in the left-luggage locker. He thought of Sammy. He would have to get in touch with him. As soon as his ankle was mended, he would have to telephone him and explain why he had had to take his savings. Sammy might be able to tell him what action Massino was taking.

He saw a movement through the open window and his hand flew to his gun. Then he relaxed as he saw Freeman coming across the clearing, carrying a burlap sack that jerked and writhed in his grasp.

Snakes!

Johnny grimaced.

What a way to earn a living!

Five minutes later, Freeman came into the bedroom, carrying two glasses of ice cold beer.

"How's the ankle?" he asked, giving Johnny one of the glasses and then sitting on the end of the bed.

"Still hurts, but nothing bad."

"I'll take a look at it in a moment." Freeman drank, sighed, then set down the half-empty glass. "I found three Cottonmouths. You've brought me luck." He smiled, "Do I ask your name, friend or would you rather I didn't?"

"Call me Johnny." A pause, then Johnny said, "Do you always treat strangers the way you're treating me?"

"You're the first. Yes, I believe in helping people when I can. A long time ago I needed a lot of help myself and someone came along and helped me. It's something I remember. Cast your bread upon the waters." Freeman chuckled. "I'm not a religious man, but that saying makes sense to me. There's one thing I've learned, living the way I do and that's not to ask questions and to accept people on face value."

"That's as good a rule as any," Johnny said quietly. "I guess I'm lucky you found me."

"Let's have a look at the ankle, then I'll help you undress. I've got a spare pair of pyjamas you can have."

Gently, he removed the bandage, soaked it in ice water, and replaced it. Then he helped Johnny out of his jacket.

Only for the briefest moment did Freeman pause when he saw the gun holster and the gun. Then he waited until Johnny unbuckled the harness and put the gun down by his side.

"That's part of my trouble," Johnny said.

"I guess it's part of a lot of people's troubles these days," Freeman said. "Let's get your pants off," and he gently drew Johnny's trousers over the injured ankle.

There was a tinkling sound and Freeman looked down. He bent and picked up something, then looked at Johnny. "Is this yours?" he asked. "It dropped out of your trousers' cuff."

He held out his open palm.

Lying in the middle of his palm was the St Christopher medal.

*　　*　　*

Johnny lay staring out of the open window at the moon-lit jungle. From the other bedroom, he could hear Freeman snoring softly. He held the St Christopher medal in his hand.

It had come back to him, he was thinking, but at what a cost!

All the time he had been searching for it, it had been in his trousers' cuff as if jeering at him! Had it not been for the medal he would have still been working for Massino, helping him in the search for the missing money! Because he panicked, believing the medal was in Andy's office, he was now on the run. He felt like throwing the medal out of the window and cursing it, but he was too superstitious to do this.

As long as you have it, nothing really bad can happen to you.

He could hear his mother's sad, weary voice as if she were in the room with him.

Well, he had it back! So maybe the organization wouldn't find him. Maybe, after all, he would have his boat. Maybe he would be the first man in history to escape the Mafia's death sentence!

He hooked the medal onto the chain and squeezed the hook tightly shut.

But lying there, watching the rising moon, listening to the sounds of the wind in the trees, the medal cold against his sweating chest, gave him no comfort.

He lay sleepless until the dawn came and then he slept and while he slept two cars, with the pick of Massino's mob, converged on the scene of the truck accident.

Lu Berilli was in charge of the operation. The cars pulled up as the sun began to climb, lighting the jungle.

Berilli surveyed the dense jungle facing him and grimaced. This, he now realized, was going to be a hell of an operation. If Johnny was hiding somewhere in these thickets, someone could get hurt, and Berilli had no stomach to come up against a man with Johnny's reputation for fast shooting. He wished he had kept his mouth shut, but it was now too late. Eight men crowded around him, waiting. They were all tough and trigger-happy: specially picked by Massino.

"This is the spot," Berilli said, trying to sound confident. "We'll split up. Three of you to the left: three to the right. Freddy, Jack and me go down the centre. Watch it? He's in there somewhere. Don't take any chances."

The two he had picked to go with him – Freddy and Jack – were button men who had worked for the Mafia and had been loaned to Massino as the New York police were hunting for them: ruthless killers, utterly without nerves.

Freddy was in his late twenties: thin, hard, dark with stony eyes and an irritating habit of whistling through his teeth. Jack was five years older than Freddy. He was a garotte artist, short, squat with restless flat eyes and an inane grin that was a fixture on his fat face.

The men split up and moved into the dark jungle.

Reaching the burned-out truck, Berilli paused.

"Some smash," he said. He looked down the path that led deeper into the jungle. "Jack, you go ahead. I follow you. Freddy keeps in the rear. Take it slow. He could be holed up anywhere in this goddamn mess."

*   *   *

Johnny came awake as Freeman opened his bedroom door. "Good night?" Freeman asked and gave Johnny a cup of tea.

"Fair." Johnny sat up and gratefully sipped the tea.

"I'm off into the jungle," Freeman said, "but I'll take a look before I go." He went out and returned with a bowl of ice water, changed the bandage, then nodded his satisfaction. "It's coming along, the inflammation has gone. I won't be back for seven or eight hours. I'll leave you some cold stew. You want a book?"

Johnny shook his head.

"I don't read books. I'll be okay."

"I'll lock you in and pull the shutters. You don't have to worry. No one ever comes here, but let's play it safe."

Johnny's fingers touched his gun.

"I'll be fine ... and thanks for everything."

With a bowl of cold rattlesnake stew by his side, a supply of cigarettes and a flask of ice water, Johnny settled down on his hard little bed. Freeman swung the heavy slatted wooden shutters closed.

"It'll be hot later," he said, "but better too hot than sorry." He seemed to sense the danger Johnny was in. "Sorry to leave you, but I've got to find a cranebrake rattler. The hospital is yelling for its serum. Could take me all day."

"I'm fine," Johnny said. "Maybe I could use a book ... anything but the Bible."

Freeman went into the living-room and, after a while, came back with a copy of *The Godfather* by Puzo.

Johnny hadn't read a book since he had left school. When he found this book was the story of the Mafia organization he became absorbed in it. Time fled away. So absorbed was he that he forgot to eat the cold stew and it wasn't until he found the light was fading as it came through the slatted shutters and he had difficulty in seeing the print that he realized he was hungry, that his ankle no longer ached and it was 17.20 by his watch.

If books are as good as this one, he thought, I've been missing something.

He was finishing the cold stew and about to light a cigarette when he heard the lock turn in the cabin door. Hurriedly, he dropped his cigarette and reached for his gun.

"It's me," Freeman called and came into the small bedroom. "I think there's trouble. There are three men heading this way. They didn't see me. They're all carrying guns."

Johnny struggled upright.

"They'll be here in ten minutes or less. Come on, Johnny, I can hide you where they won't think of looking." Freeman hoisted Johnny up on his left foot. "You hop. Don't put any weight on your bad foot."

Johnny grabbed up his gun and holster, then supported by Freeman, he hopped through the living-room and out into the sunshine. Freeman steered him to the big lean-to behind the cabin.

"This is my snake house," Freeman said. "You don't have to be scared. They're all in cages and can't touch you."

He manoeuvred Johnny into the semi-darkness and Johnny could hear the dry rattling sound a rattlesnake makes when alarmed. Freeman propped him up against the wall, then moving to a big eight-foot-high cage, he dragged it forward. Johnny saw the cage was alive with writhing rattlesnakes. Freeman caught hold of him and got him behind the cage and propped him against the wall.

"You'll be okay," he said. "Don't worry. I'll fix the bed. They won't know you're here," then he moved the cage back on Johnny, wedging him against the wall and out of sight.

Johnny could smell the snakes. Their movements chilled him. Leaning hard on his sound foot, keeping his injured foot slightly off the ground, he set himself to wait.

Berilli, flanked on either side by Freddy and Jack suddenly came on the clearing and Freeman's cabin.

For hours now they had combed the jungle and they were sick and tired of the search. They had become careless. Berilli had realized after three or four hours that Johnny could be lying, hidden, in any of the big thickets and by keeping still, they could have walked past him.

He realized this operation had been too hastily mounted. What they needed in this goddamn place was a dog to flush Johnny out. But now he was stuck with the operation and he was scared to go back to Massino and report no success.

He, Freddy and Jack had walked through the jungle for six gruelling hours. The only thing they had seen that moved was a snake. Then just when Berilli was about to call off the operation and admit defeat, they came on the clearing and the log cabin.

The three instinctively dodged back behind a thicket.

"He could be here," Berilli said.

They started across the clearing at the cabin, then they saw a tall, thin man, wearing shabby khaki drill come out of the cabin. He walked over to the well and began drawing water.

"Jack ... you talk to him," Berilli said.

"Not me, pal," Jack said. "You chat him up ... I'll cover you."

"So will I," Freddy said and grinned. "You're the boss, Lu."

So Berilli moved out of the clearing, his heart thumping, wondering if Johnny was holed up in the cabin, taking aim at him through the slatted shutters.

Freeman looked up as Berilli approached him.

"Hi, stranger." His voice was soft and calm. "Have you lost your way? I haven't seen anyone this way for months."

Berilli eyed him, keeping his gun behind him, out of sight.

"You live here?" he demanded.

"That's right." Freeman was perfectly at ease. "Jay Freeman: I'm the snake man."

Berilli stiffened.

"Snakes? What do you mean?"

Patiently, Freeman explained.

"I collect serum for hospitals." He paused, looking directly into Berilli's suspicious eyes. "Who are you?"

"Have you seen a short, thick-set man with black hair, around forty years of age? We're looking for him."

"As I said, you're the first human I've seen in months."

Berilli looked uneasily at the cabin.

"You'd better not lie to me. If he's in there, you're in trouble and I mean trouble."

"What's all this about?" Freeman asked mildly. "Are you the police?"

Ignoring the question, Berilli signalled to the other two who came out from behind the thicket.

"We'll take a look at your cabin," he said to Freeman as Jack and Freddy joined him. "Go ahead, bright boy, and stop flapping with your mouth."

Freeman walked into the cabin. Using him as a shield, Berilli entered behind him, his gun in hand, his heart pounding, while Jack and Freddy waited outside. After a quick search, pushing Freeman always ahead of him, Berilli came out of the cabin and into the sunshine. He shook his head at the other two.

"What is that?" he demanded, seeing the lean-to.

"My snake house," Freeman said. "Have a look. I've just caught a cranebrake rattler. Have you ever seen one?"

Crouched behind the snake cage, Johnny heard every word and he thumbed back the safety on his gun. He could hear a soft whistling sound and he knew who was out there: Freddy, a Mafia killer and more dangerous than any of the snakes, writhing and rattling around him.

"Go ahead," Berilli said and prodded Freeman with his gun.

Again sheltering behind Freeman, Berilli peered into the lean-to, saw the cages, smelt the snake smell and backed away.

He crossed over to Freddy and Jack.

"Let's get out of here," he said. "We could search this goddamn jungle for months and still not find him."

"That's the brightest thing you've said so far," Jack said.

Freeman watched the three men move off into the jungle, then he fetched a bucket of water from the well and returned to his cabin. He waited some ten minutes, then leaving the cabin, he moved into the jungle as quietly and as swiftly as one of his snakes. Without being seen or heard, he caught up with the three men and watched them meet up with six other men, watched them talk, then saw them get into two cars and drive away.

Then he returned to his cabin to release Johnny from his hiding-place and assure him the hunt was over.

6

For eight, long boring days, Johnny remained in Freeman's cabin. During this time his beard made progress and his ankle mended.

Looking at himself in the mirror in the shower room, he saw how the beard altered his appearance and he felt confident, unless he was examined closely, that no one would recognize him. He had got Freeman to drive into town and buy him two sets of khaki drill, a bush jacket and a bush hat, together with toilet things, shirts, socks and a suitcase.

Although, from time to time, his ankle still ached, he could now walk fairly well and he felt it was time to move on. He decided to pick up a south-bound truck on the freeway and make his way to Jackson. He was sure Fuselli would give him shelter for a time, and then when the heat had cooled off, he would go back and collect the money. By that time, his grey-black beard would be impressive and he felt the risk of returning had to be taken. With some of the money he had taken from Sammy, he would buy a used car, and still have plenty in hand.

But first, he must have information.

So on the eighth day, now dressed in khaki drill and wearing the bush hat, he asked Freeman to drive him into town.

"I've got to make a phone call," he explained.

Johnny hadn't seen much of Freeman during his stay at the cabin. The snake man went off at dawn and seldom got back until dusk. They then spent a couple of hours together over supper and then both went to bed. But during those hours, Freeman never asked questions, talked easily about every subject under the sun and encouraged Johnny to read, and Johnny discovered the magic of books. The books he liked best were books on travel and sailing and Freeman had a good selection.

"Sure," Freeman said. "Are you thinking of leaving? You can stay here as long as you like, Johnny."

"I've got to get on."

"I'll miss you."

This was the nicest thing anyone had ever said to Johnny and to hide his emotion, he gave Freeman a light punch on his arm.

"Yeah ... that makes two of us, and I won't forget what you've done for me. Now listen, I've plenty of money. I want you to have two hundred for all you've done for me. Buy yourself a telly or something to remember me by."

Freeman laughed.

"Appreciated but not accepted. That's one thing I never need ... money. You keep it. You may need it ... I won't."

They drove into town early the following morning. Johnny felt naked and his eyes darted continuously to right and left. Under his bush jacket was his gun and he kept fingering the butt. But he saw no one suspicious. He went into the small hotel and shut himself in a call booth. He looked at his watch: the time was 08.10. Sammy should be getting up by now. He dialled the number and waited.

Sammy answered almost immediately.

"Sammy ... this is Johnny."

He heard Sammy catch his breath.

"I – I don't want to talk to you, Mr Johnny. You could get me into bad trouble. I've got nothing to say to you."

"Listen!" Johnny put a snap in his voice. "You're my friend, Sammy ... remember? I've done a lot for you ... now it's your turn."

He heard Sammy moan softly and he could imagine him, sweating, grey-faced and trembling.

"Yeah. What is it, Mr Johnny? You took all my money. That wasn't nice. You're in real bad, and if they knew you were talking to me, I'd be in real bad too."

"They won't know. Sammy ... I had to have that money. You'll get it back. I promise. Don't worry about it. Are they looking for me?"

"They sure are! This Mr Tanza is handling it! I heard the boss and Mr Tanza talking while I was driving them. I don't know where you are and I don't want to know, but they're looking for you in Florida. They talked of someone called Fuselli. Toni and Ernie are out there. You've got to be careful, Mr Johnny."

Johnny stiffened. So the heat really was on! How the hell had Massino got on to Fuselli?

"Have you gone crazy, Mr Johnny?" Sammy went on, his voice husky. "You really took all that money? I can't believe it! Mr Joe is like he's demented. I'd sooner collect than drive him. He scares me to death the way he acts!"

"I'll call you in a little while, Sammy," Johnny said quietly. "Keep your ears open. Don't worry about your money ... you'll get it back. Just listen to everything the boss says. I need your help."

"Mr Johnny, please keep away from me. If they find out ...please, Mr Johnny. You keep my money. Just keep away from me," and Sammy hung up.

Johnny stood motionless in the stuffy booth, staring out into the lounge of the hotel, feeling his heart beating heavily and a chill of fear down his spine. By going to Fuselli as he had planned, he could have walked into a trap. Now he really was on his own.

Leaving the booth, he went out into the sunshine and got in the car by Freeman's side.

"Okay?" Freeman asked as he started the motor.

Johnny thought of Carlo Tanza. This meant the Mafia organization were now hunting for him and they had somehow guessed he was heading south. They had somehow got on to Fuselli. He had a feeling of being in a net. For a moment, the net was above him and around him, but he still had room to manoeuvre.

"Not so good," he said and lit a cigarette. "Don't worry your brains about me. I'll move on tonight."

Freeman glanced at him, then drove back to the cabin in silence.

When the two men entered the cabin, Freeman said, "Look Johnny, two heads are better than one. Do you feel like talking or do you still want to handle this on your own?"

For a brief moment, Johnny was tempted to pour out the whole story, then he thought of the danger Freeman could be in. If the Mafia even suspected he had hidden here, they would torture Freeman until he talked, then kill him.

"I'll handle it," he said. "You keep out of it."

"As bad as that?" Freeman looked searchingly at him.

"That's it ... as bad as that."

"You'll come out of it, Johnny. There's something about you ... guts ... I don't know, but I'll put my money on you."

"Not too much," Johnny said and forced a smile. "I'd hate you to lose it." He went into his room, shut the door and lay on the bed.

What was he to do? he asked himself. He longed to go south, but if they knew that was where he was heading, wouldn't it be asking for trouble? He considered this. On the face of it, it would be risking a lot, but maybe the risk was worth it. Maybe, after a while, they would decide he hadn't gone south after all and start looking elsewhere. Anyway, wherever he went they would be hunting for him and he wanted so badly to go south.

For an hour or so, he lay there, experiencing a sick feeling of being trapped, then a tap came on the door and Freeman came in.

"I've work to do, Johnny," he said. "I won't be back until late. Why not stay on here?"

"No." Johnny got off the bed. "It'll work out as you said. I'll be gone by the time you get back. I want to say thanks." He stared for a long moment at Freeman. "You may not know it, but I'd be dead by now but for you."

"I didn't know it was that bad. Those three men ..."

Johnny held out his hand.

"The less you know ..."

The two men shook hands. There was a pause, then Freeman went away. Through the window, Johnny watched him striding into the jungle, carrying his sack.

So what was he going to do now? He fingered his St. Christopher medal. Why wait until dark? Why not go now? He felt the urge to get out of this suffocating jungle and on to the freeway. He took out his gun, checked it, then slid it back into its holster. Then he picked up his suitcase, looked around the little room, feeling a pang of loneliness to be leaving it, then walked out into the sunshine and started down the jungle path that would eventually bring him to the freeway.

It took him half an hour to get out of the jungle and to the freeway. This long walk made his ankle ache. Once on the freeway, he kept on, limping a little until he was some two miles from Freeman's cabin. Then he paused, leaning against a tree and watched the traffic roar by.

Trucks, cars and cars pulling caravans roared by him. He decided to start walking again. By now his ankle was throbbing and he wondered, with a feeling of alarm, if he had been too confident about his injury. He stopped in the shade and as he was about to sit on the grass to rest an open truck came to a stop some twenty yards from him.

Grabbing up his suitcase, he limped up to the truck. The driver had got out and had the hood up. He was staring at the engine.

As Johnny approached the man, he looked hard at him: tall, lean, around twenty-seven years of age with long nut-brown hair, wearing dirty overalls, and to Johnny, harmless enough.

"You in trouble?" Johnny asked as he reached the truck.

The man looked up.

An odd face, Johnny thought. Thin, narrow eyes, a small mouth, a thin nose and a sour expression which Johnny had often seen: a defeated face.

"Never out of it. I live in trouble. Just a goddamn plug." He stood away from the truck and lit a cigarette. "Got to let her cool off. You looking for a ride?"

Johnny set down his suitcase.

"Yeah. Where are you heading?"

"Little Creek. That's my home. This side of New Symara."

"I pay my way," Johnny said.

The man looked sharply at him, eyeing Johnny's new khaki drill, his new bush hat.

"Is that right?"

"Ten dollars." Johnny knew when a man needed money. He had seen that expression over and over again.

"Sure friend, I'll take you. Ten dollars, huh?"

Johnny felt in his pocket and produced a ten dollar bill.

"Let's pay in advance, then we can forget it."

Lean, long fingers took the bill.

"I'll change the plug. You get in, friend."

Ten minutes later, the man swung himself into the cab beside Johnny.

"I'm Ed Scott," he said as he started the motor.

"Johnny Bianco," Johnny said.

The truck began to roar down the freeway.

"What's your racket, Ed?" Johnny asked after a mile or two of silence.

"I haul shrimps." Scott gave a harsh, bitter laugh. "Every goddamn day except Sunday. I pick up a hundred crates of shrimps and rush them to Richville: that's a hundred and twenty mile haul: two hundred and forty there and back. In this truck I do it in four hours: so that's eight hours of my day, sitting here, driving. I have to get up at five to load up. I don't get back home until seven. I've a three-year contract with four top-class Richville restaurants: they use shrimps the way a bucket full of holes uses water. I thought I'd found Eldorado when I got this contract, but, man! is it a killer!"

Johnny was listening. He thought: what a way to earn a living!

"Goddamn it!" Scott went on. "I should have my head examined! Freda warned me ... my wife. You know something? I don't listen to women. Women are all piss and wind. They yak for the sake of hearing their own voices. But after eight months of this, I'm beginning to think Freda has more sense than me. A year ago I was hauling for the Florida Citrus people. That paid steady, and it wasn't hard, but I have this bug: I can't work with people. When some punk of an overseer starts sounding off, I flip my lid. I have to work on my own and for myself." He glanced at Johnny. "You with me or aren't you?"

"I'm with you," Johnny said quietly. He took out his pack of cigarettes. "Smoke?"

"Why not?"

Johnny lit two cigarettes and passed one to Scott.

"So I've saved some money and I bought this truck and I think I'm in business." Scott went on. "I say I'll haul anything. So okay, I get landed with this shrimp contract. There's no let up. I've got to get these goddamn shrimps up to Richville every day or they can sue the pants off me. And what do I get out of it? That's what Freda asked and I wouldn't listen to her. So ... I've found out. I clear a hundred and fifty bucks a week. That has to take care of me, my wife, repairs to the truck, the rent and all the other extras and I'm now finding I'm working my goddamn tail off for peanuts."

"You have yourself a tough deal," Johnny said.

"You can say that again." There was a long pause, then Scott said, "And you? What's your racket?"

"Call me a bum," Johnny said. "For years I've been a rent-collector and suddenly I could take it no more. I sold up everything I owned: my car, a TV. set, stuff ... you know and I'm here. I've lived north all my life. So I've come south. When my money runs out, I'll get a job, but not until my money runs out."

"You've got no wife?"

"No."

"Yeah ... a man is free without a woman. You're lucky. Get a woman and you have to work."

"You got kids?"

"I wanted a couple but Freda's against it. I guess, now looking back, she was right. The way we live ... no place for kids."

"There's time ... you're young."

Scott laughed. "I guess, but they won't come now. Not on this shrimp haul."

He lapsed into moody silence. Tired by his walk and lulled by the roar of the engine, Johnny dozed off. He slept for half an hour, then came awake with a start. The truck was pounding down the freeway: on either side were mangrove trees and jungle. He glanced at Scott, saw his sweat-glistening, exhausted face and saw the tension in his hands and arms as he held the wheel.

"Suppose you let me drive?" Johnny said, "and you take a nap? What's the matter with that?"

"Could you handle her?" Scott looked hopefully at Johnny.

"I can handle anything on four wheels."

Scott slowed, pulled onto the verge and stopped the truck. "Could I sleep!" he said. "You keep going. When you see a signpost marked Eastling, wake me up. Okay?"

"Nothing to it." They exchanged seats, and even before Johnny had started the truck, Scott was asleep.

So Johnny drove, careful not to exceed the speed limit, aware that if some maniac caused an accident, he would be in more trouble. Suddenly, after eight days in hiding, with nothing to do, he felt relaxed. He was now doing a job and he realized that was what he wanted to do.

He thought about what Scott had told him. Eight hours a day in this hot truck and the pay off: one hundred and fifty dollars! His mind shifted to all that money waiting for him in the left-luggage locker! $186,000! But when would he get it? Would he ever get it? The organization was now looking for him! That meant hundreds of people throughout the south who had some connection with the Mafia would be warned to look out for him. One never knew who was employed by the Mafia and who wasn't, but he was certain that there would be always someone in a bar, a café, even a garage, a cheap eating-house, a cheap hotel, a motel who might have Mafia connections. When he finally reached Little Creek which Scott had said was where he lived, what was he to do? A sudden stranger! Even with his beard, he would be investigated. He was sure, knowing how the Mafia worked, there would be a reward out for him. He looked at the sleeping man lolling in the corner of the cab. Very few brains there, he thought. An individualist: a man who had worked on his own because he couldn't submit to discipline. Johnny understood that, but because of this failing, this man had got himself into a rat race that made him less than a slave.

Johnny switched his mind from his own troubles and thought about what Scott had told him. He got up at 05.00, loaded up crates of shrimps, then belted up the freeway, four hours there, four hours back, got home at 19.00, in time for dinner, a look at the telly and then bed: six days a week for one hundred and fifty dollars! At the present cost of living, what did that mean?

Suddenly, he could smell the sea. He sniffed at it the way a woman will sniff at an outrageously expensive perfume. The Sea! His mind flashed to a white, beautiful forty-five footer ... his! Once he had got all this money, waiting for him in the left-luggage locker, he would go to some ship builder and talk boats. His heart beat excitedly as he imagined the moment when he had signed the papers, paid the money, then walked on the gang plank and on to the deck. His! Then he thought of the danger: going back, getting those two heavy bags out of the left-luggage locker, then getting out of town. Not yet! He would have to be patient. He would have to remain in hiding until the heat had really cooled off. Patience! Discipline! He would do it. Suddenly he felt confident. Sooner or later, Massino and the Mafia Dons would get bored trying to find him. He would keep in touch with Sammy who would alert him of any danger. When Sammy finally told him that the heat was off, then he would go back, but not before.

Ahead of him, he saw the signpost: Eastling, and he slowed down. Reaching across, he shook Scott awake.

"Here we are," he said. "Eastling."

"Pull over and stop," Scott said, shaking himself awake. "Phew! Seems only five minutes." He dug sleep out of his eyes. "I'll take her."

They changed seats.

"Would there be somewhere for me to sleep?" Johnny asked.

Scott looked at him.

"I've a spare room: cost you five bucks a day and all found. Want it?"

"You have yourself a deal," Johnny said.

Scott engaged gear and drove the truck on to the freeway.

*   *   *

116

While Johnny was driving Scott's truck, Massino was holding a meeting in his office. Present were Carlo Tanza and Andy Lucas.

Massino had just explained to Tanza that the lead they had on this old guy Giovanni Fuselli was a wash-out. It was only with difficulty that Massino contained his rage and he kept glaring at Andy who had been responsible for this waste of time.

"What we've got to remember is Johnny didn't have the money with him when he left town," Massino said. "It was Andy's idea he was working with someone else and we thought it could be this Fuselli, but it wasn't. Toni and Ernie are sure Fuselli is clean. So ... one of two things. Either Johnny was working with someone we don't know about or he panicked and left the money stashed somewhere in town." He looked at Tanza. "What do you think?"

"There's a third possibility," Tanza said. "He could have put those two bags on a Greyhound bus. The station is right across the street. No problem there for him. You buy a ticket, stick the bags on a bus and they'll deliver to any Greyhound station on their route. I know that's what I would have done. I wouldn't have been nutty enough to stash the money here where I would have to come back for it, and from what I know about Bianda, he's far from nutty."

"You don't think he was working with someone?"

Tanza shrugged.

"Doesn't seem likely. He's a loner ... the only friend he seems to have had is this smoke, Sammy the Black and he wouldn't have the guts to steal chewing gum from a kid. Yeah, seems to me that's what Bianda did. Grabbed the money, rushed it across to the bus station, got the bags on a bus, knowing they would be delivered to await arrival, then he went back to his whore, found he had lost his medal, flipped his lid and beat it out of town."

"We can check," Massino said. He looked at Andy. "At that time there would be very few buses leaving. Get over there and check. Someone should remember if two heavy bags were put on a bus."

Andy nodded and left the office.

Massino looked at Tanza.

"He's now been gone eight days." His little eyes were like red beads. "Think you can find him?"

Tanza grinned evilly.

"We always find them, but it costs."

"So how much?"

"Depends on how long it takes. Let's say fifty per cent of the take."

Massino said softly, "I want him alive. You'll get fifty per cent if he's delivered to me alive. A third if he's dead."

"He could be tricky to take alive."

Massino closed his huge fists.

"I want him alive! I'm going to smash that sonofabitch to pulp with my own hands." His rage gave him an insane look and even Tanza who was ruthless and tough was shocked. "So get after him! Get your wonderful organization hunting him!" Massino slammed his fists down on the desk. His voice rose to a snarling shout. "I don't give a goddamn what it costs! I want him!"

* * *

"Nearly home," Scott said, slowing the truck. "A mile ahead and to the left is New Symara ... that's where I load. Up here," he swung the truck off the freeway and driving slowly climbed a narrow, sandy road, bordered either side with dense stands of pines, "leads to Little Creek. It's little enough. A store, around a dozen cabins and the lake. We've got a houseboat on the far side of the lake. No one bothers us. People in Little Creek are too busy to earn a dollar to bother anyone."

This was reassuring news to Johnny.

The sandy track was now edged with thistles, ferns and blue flags. The jungle behind was so thick it looked like a black curtain to Johnny.

They came out suddenly on to the lake. Johnny judged it to be a mile and a half across. There were several boats out with men fishing. One of the men raised his hand in a salute as Scott drove by. Scott waved back.

"Supper time," he said with a crooked grin. "Everyone here fishes for their suppers and their goddamn dinners too. I wonder if Freda's caught anything."

Leaving the group of cabins behind them, they drove for a mile through the jungle, then came out suddenly into a cleared space where Johnny saw a long, shabby houseboat with a twenty-foot-long, battered pier joining it to the mainland.

"Lived here for two years," Scott said as he drove the truck into a parking bay, covered with tatty bamboo. "Got it for a song. Had to work on it, but now it's not too bad. You reckon to stay long?"

Johnny turned and looked directly at Scott.

"Doesn't that depend on what your wife says? She may not want a stranger hanging around."

Scott shrugged.

"You don't have to worry about Freda: she's as money hungry as I am. I can use thirty-five bucks a week and she can use some company. Not much fun for her being left here all alone all day."

119

Johnny continued to look directly at Scott.

"Just a minute ... Is there something wrong with your wife? Is she a cripple or something?"

"No... what do you mean?"

"Come on, Scott," Johnny said impatiently, "grow up! Why should your wife want a man here ... it's lonely enough. Doesn't it worry you?"

"Why should it?" Scott said. "If you think you can lay her, go ahead. If she has you, you're welcome. I haven't touched her that way since we married." He leered. "I get all the loving I need in Richville and I don't need a lot. When a guy works the way I do, once a month is all he needs."

"What's it between you two then?" Johnny asked, startled.

"Forget it." Scott swung himself out of the cab. "If you want to stay, then stay as long as you like so long as you pay. Come on, I'll show you your room."

As they walked across the pier, Scott paused and pointed.

"There she is ... swimming. Spends most of her time in the lake."

Johnny screwed up his eyes against the reflection of the sun on the still water. He saw a head bobbing in the water, some three hundred yards from the houseboat.

Scott put two fingers in his mouth and emitted a shrill whistle. A hand come out of the water in a wave.

"Come on in," Scott said.

There was a good wide deck around the houseboat and together they entered a long, low living-room shabbily furnished, but comfortable enough. There was a TV set in one corner.

"Here's your room," Scott said and opened the door. "Dump your things and have a swim. We swim raw. You don't have to bother about Freda. She's seen more naked men than I've seen shrimps."

Johnny looked around the tiny room. There was a bed, a closet, a night-table and a chair. The window looked onto the lake. It was all clean and he liked it.

"This is fine."

"It's okay."

Scott left him.

Johnny looked out of the window. He would have liked to have swum, but not naked. He saw Scott come out on deck, naked and dive into the lake. He watched him swim to the blonde head, pause and after a minute or so, swim on. The blonde head headed towards the houseboat.

Johnny stood by the window and watched. He kept out of sight, peering around the curtain as the woman swung herself on to the deck. She was tall, brown-bodied and naked. She had long legs, tight, firm breasts and as she turned and walked along the deck, Johnny watched her heavy buttocks roll. His eyes had been too busy looking at her body to see her face except to notice her wet, blonde hair reached to the middle of her shoulders.

Johnny wiped the sweat off his face. What had he walked into? he asked himself. This was all woman: the most sensual, sexual body he had seen.

He now felt in urgent need of cold water. Stripping off, keeping on his underpants, he stepped out onto the deck and dived into the lake.

The cool water gave him pleasure. He was a powerful swimmer and he swam for some two hundred yards in a racing stroke to release the stiffness and the lust the woman had raised in him, then he turned around and swam back, joining Scott as he was swinging himself up onto the deck.

"I'll get you a towel," Scott said and disappeared into the living-room. He returned moments later, tossed Johnny a towel, then disappeared again.

Johnny mopped off, then went to his bedroom. He smelt onions frying and his mouth watered. He realized he hadn't eaten since he had left the snake man's cabin and suddenly he was starving.

Dressed, he left his room and went into the living-room. Scott was smoking and staring out of the window. He looked up as Johnny came in.

"Okay?"

"Fine."

"We don't drink here," Scott said. "Can't afford it. If you want a drink you can buy anything at the store. Take the motorboat over tomorrow."

Johnny would have liked a whisky, but he sat down, shrugging.

"That smells good."

"Yeah. Freda can cook."

"You told her about me?"

"Oh, sure." Scott leaned forward and turned to the TV. set. "She's in the kitchen." He waved. "Go talk to her."

Johnny hesitated, then getting to his feet, he pushed open a door at the far end of the living-room and looked into the small kitchen with a butane gas cooker, a cupboard, a table, a refrigerator and Freda Scott.

She was stirring something in a pan and she looked up. Johnny felt a little jolt. God! he thought, this woman's beautiful!

And she was. Her face matched her body. She had to be a Swede with those bright china blue eyes, the blonde, silky hair, the high cheekbones, the straight, long nose.

While he stared at her, she gave him a brief, quick searching look, then scooping up raw, chopped-up fish, she dropped the pieces into the pan.

"Hungry?" She had a musical, soft voice which was like a sexual caress. "I guess you must be. Well, it won't be long. Ed says you're going to stay."

"If it's all right with you."

She was wearing a pair of stretch pants and a man's shirt, a faded blue. He eyed the curve of her buttocks, remembering the body, naked. His eyes shifted to her full breasts, straining against the shirt.

"We want the money," she said. "Anyway, as Ed says, it'll be company for me. Do you like curry?"

"I like anything."

"Go watch TV. It'll be twenty minutes. I prefer to cook on my own."

She glanced up and they looked at each other. The bright blue eyes ran over his short, heavily-built body, then to his face and their eyes locked.

"Call me Johnny," Johnny said and his voice was a little husky.

"Freda." She waved him away. "Keep Ed company ... not that he likes company, but he might grow used to it." Johnny caught a bitter note in her voice.

Leaving her, he returned to the living-room.

*   *   *

Andy Lucas came into Massino's office, closed the door and looked from Massino to Tanza. The room was heavy with cigar smoke and there was a half-bottle of whisky, glasses and an ice bucket on the desk.

"Well?" Massino snarled.

"I've checked," Andy said. "It's taken time, but I've now talked with every driver who left the bus station between 2 a.m. and 5 a.m. on the night of the steal. None of them took those bags. If they take luggage, they have to issue a ticket ... no luggage."

"So that thins it down," Tanza said. "He either had someone with him who took the money out or the money is still in town."

Massino brooded about this.

"So suppose he was on his own. Suppose he dumped the money in one of those left-luggage lockers across the street, planning to come back for it? What do you think?"

Tanza shook his head.

"He's no fool. He must know he couldn't come back. It's my bet he was working with someone who took the money out."

Massino nodded.

"Looks like it, but just suppose he did dump the money in one of those lockers." He looked at Andy. "Can we check?"

"There are over three hundred lockers," Andy said. "Even the Commissioner couldn't get into them all without a judge's say-so. We could try, but do you want that, Mr Joe?"

Massino thought about this, then shook his head. "No. You're right. We start a caper like that and the press will get on to it." He thought some more. "But we can seal off those lockers. Get it organized, Andy. I want a twenty-four-hour watch kept. Have two men on four-hour shifts, day and night, watching those lockers. Give them a description of the bags. If anyone opens a locker and takes those bags, he's to be nailed!"

Andy nodded and left the office.

"So what's the organization doing?" Massino demanded.

"Take it easy, Joe. We'll find him ... may take a little time, but we'll find him. The word's gone out. By now, everyone connected with us knows we want him. Take a look at this." He produced from his wallet a printer's proof and laid it on the desk. "This will appear in all the Florida newspapers tomorrow morning."

Massino leaned forward and read the proof.

HAVE YOU SEEN THIS MAN?
$10,000 Reward

Below this headline was Johnny's prison photograph. The letterpress went on:

Missing from home, believed suffering from loss of memory: Johnny Bianda. Heavily built, five foot nine inches, clean shaven, sallow complexion, grey-black hair, forty-two years of age. Known to favour a St Christopher medal.

A reward of $10,000 will be paid to anyone giving information that will lead to this man being found.

Contact: Dyson & Dyson, Attorneys-at-Law, 1600 Crew Street.

East City. Tel. 007.611.09

"He'll hide up with someone without money ... they always do," Tanza said with his evil grin. "If this doesn't flush him out, we have other tricks, but I think it will."

7

Johnny came fully awake when he heard the phut-phut of a motorboat. Lifting his head, he looked out of the open window to see Freda in a small boat, powered by an outboard motor, moving away from the houseboat. She was wearing the faded shirt and stretch pants and a cigarette dangled from her lips. The boat headed across the lake. Johnny dropped back on his pillow. He had been woken previously by the sound of the truck starting up, and only half conscious, he realized Scott was off to work.

He lay on the small bed and thought of the previous evening. They had eaten curried Black Crappie, a lake fish, with rice, onions and tomatoes. It had been a good meal, eaten more or less in silence. Scott had wanted to see something on TV and he had eaten fast, then leaving the other two at the table, he had gone over to the set and turned it on.

Johnny had been very aware of Freda as they sat opposite each other. He had eaten hungrily.

"You cook fine," he said.

"Ed says the same." The flat in her voice made him look sharply at her. "That's all men think of ... food."

He glanced across the room to where Scott was absorbed in the lighted screen.

"Not all men."

"Have some more."

"I'd be nuts if I didn't."

She pushed back her chair.

"We live like pigs here. Go ahead. I've things to do," and she left the table, going into the kitchen.

The food was so good and he was so hungry, he didn't hesitate. He cleared the bowl, then sat back reaching for a cigarette.

After a short smoke, he crushed out his cigarette, collected the plates and carried them into the kitchen. He was surprised to see her sitting on the deck, staring across the lake.

"Let's clear up," he said. "You want to?"

"Sounds like you're domesticated." There was a slight jeer in her voice. "Leave it for tomorrow ... tomorrow's another day."

"I'll do it. You stay there."

She stared at him, then shrugged.

"So I stay here."

It took him some twenty minutes to wash the dishes and clear the table. He liked doing this. It reminded him of the safety of his own apartment which seemed far away, then he joined her on the deck and sat beside her in an old, creaking bamboo chair.

"Nice view," he said.

"You think so? I've got used to it. After two years, a view gets faded. Where are you from?"

"Up north ... and you?"

"Sweden."

"I guessed that. Your hair ... your eyes ... you're a long way from home."

"Yes." A pause, then she said, "Look, you don't have to make conversation with me. For two years I've lived more or less on my own. I'm used to it. You're our lodger. I wouldn't have you here if it wasn't for the money. I like being alone."

"I won't get in your way." He stood up. "I've had a rough day. I'm turning in. Thank you for a fine meal."

She leaned back in her chair and looked up at him.

"Thanks for clearing up."

They regarded each other, then he went into the living-room. The TV serial had come to an end and Scott was getting to his feet.

"Bed," he said. "See you around seven tomorrow evening. You got all you want? The fishing tackle is in that closet there. Use my rod if you want to."

"I'll do that." A pause. "Well, good night, I guess I could sleep the clock around."

Johnny went to his room and got into bed. He lay watching the moon and the still waters of the lake and he thought of Scott and his woman. Then his mind switched to Massino. He drew in a long, relaxed breath. Here, he felt safe. This surely was the one place on earth where the organization would never think to look for him.

And now after a good sleep, with the sun up, seeing Freda in the motorboat, he became fully awake. He stripped off and plunged into the lake, swam for some minutes in the cool clear water, then returned to the houseboat, dried off, dressed and went into the kitchen. Freda had set out a pot of coffee, a cup and saucer, sugar and milk. There was a stale loaf of bread and a toaster, but he didn't bother with that. He carried the cup of coffee on to the deck and sat down, looking at the distant pines, the reflections of the clouds in the lake, the stillness of the water and he felt at peace.

After drinking the coffee and smoking a cigarette, he explored the houseboat, finding it consisted of three small bedrooms, beside the living-room, the kitchen and a shower room. The bedroom next to his was obviously Freda's. The room was neat and clean with a small, single bed, a chest of drawers, a closet, books and a table with a bedside light. The room next to hers belonged to Scott: not so tidy, no books and the bed also small. In one corner stood a .22 target rifle and a shot gun. Johnny eyed these two weapons, then backed out of the room, closing the door.

He collected Scott's fishing rod and went out onto the deck. He spent the next hour trying to catch fish but he had no luck. Still, it was relaxing to sit in the sun, the rod in his hand and he thought of all that money stashed away in the left-luggage locker. If he could stay here for a week or so, he decided it would be safe to return and get the money. Surely, after six weeks, the heat would be off. In a week or so, he would go with Scott to Richville and from there call Sammy who would be able tell him what was happening.

Another hour drifted while he thought of the moment when he would buy his boat, then he heard the phut-phut of the returning motorboat and out of the sun, he saw Freda at the tiller. He waved at her and she lifted her hand. Ten minutes later she climbed on deck while Johnny secured the boat.

"You'll never catch anything from here," she said, seeing the rod. "If you want to fish, take the boat." She had a loaded shopping basket. "Lunch in two hours. Take the boat and see if you can get something for supper."

Johnny had stripped off his shirt and suddenly she looked at his hairy chest and pointed.

"What's that?"

He fingered the St Christopher medal.

"My lucky charm." He grinned. "St Christopher. My mother gave it to me. Know what she said just before she died? She said, 'As long as you have that nothing really bad can happen to you'."

"You're an Italian, aren't you?"

"That's right, but I was born in Florida."

"Well, don't lose it," and she carried the basket into the kitchen.

Taking the rod and tackle, he got in the motorboat and started the engine. It was good to be in a boat again, and an hour later when he had landed a four-pound bass, he decided he hadn't spent a nicer morning since he was a kid.

He felt absurdly proud of himself when he carried the bass into the kitchen and saw Freda's look of surprise.

"You're quite a fisherman!" she said. "Put it down there. I'll attend to it."

"I've gutted it ... used to fish a lot when I was a kid: hadn't much else to eat. That smells good."

"Ed gets a free meal in Richville. I thought I'd spend some of your money." She looked at him. "Beef casserole. Like to give me some rent? I've spent all I had."

"Why, sure." He went into his bedroom, unlocked the suitcase and took out two ten dollar bills. Then returning, he handed them to her.

"Thanks." She put the money in a shabby little purse. "We can eat."

While they were eating, she asked, "What do you plan to do? Just sit around here?"

"If I'm not in the way. I'm taking a vacation and this suits me fine."

"You're easy to please." The bitter note in her voice made him glance at her.

"Yeah, I can guess it gets monotonous after a time. Ed was telling me about this shrimp contract."

130

"He's crazy!" She forked beef into her mouth. "The moment I can lay my hands on some money, I'm off! God! I'm sick of this way of life, but we're stuck for money."

"It's tough. He seems to work like a slave. I'm sorry."

"He works all right, but does he kid himself! He'll never be anything. There are finks who slave themselves to death and never amount to anything ... he's one of them." The bright blue eyes met his. "What do you do for a living?"

"Rent collecting. I got fed up with it, sold everything and when my money runs out, I'm going to get a job on a boat. I'm crazy about boats."

"Boats?" She grimaced. "What sort of living can you make out of boats? Fishing? Is that a living?"

"A living doesn't worry me. I just want to get on a boat." She laid down her knife and fork.

"Some ambition."

"And you? If you had enough money to get away from here, what would you do?"

"Live! I'm twenty-six. I know men go for me." She stared directly at him. "You go for me, don't you?"

"So what's that to do with it?"

"If I could get to Miami, I'd find a man and I'd squeeze every dollar out of him for services rendered. You know something? I thought this was the golden land of opportunity when I landed here three years ago. Was I green? I spent two months in New York in a Travel Agency, routing old jerks to Sweden. God! Was that a bore! Then I got a transfer down to Jacksonville: the same old bore. Then one day ... my unlucky day... when I was fed to my back teeth, I had to run into Ed, full of plans of starting up in the haulage business, owning his own truck, in a year owning two trucks, in four years a fleet of trucks ... really in the money! So I married him! Okay, I asked for it and got it! We came here. 'Give me a year,' he said, 'and you'll see.

131

Let's rough it for a year, then I'll get another truck.' That's two years ago! And what a man! What a man to live with!" She looked directly at Johnny. "Are you on to him?"

"What does that mean?"

"He's kinky. High heels and whips. So we sleep apart. He gets his fun in Richville and I get my fun fishing!"

Johnny lifted his hands and let them fall heavily on his knees.

"I'm sorry."

"Don't be." She got to her feet. "Come on, lodger. You want me and I need a man. This time it's for free. Next time, it'll cost you. I've got to save money and get out of here or I'll damn well drown myself."

Johnny remained seated.

"I want you, Freda, but not on those terms," he said, quietly. "I've never paid for it and I never will."

She stared at him, then she smiled.

"I think I'm going to like you, Johnny," she said. "I think you're all man. No conditions ... let's see how good you really are."

He got up and putting his arm around her waist, cupping her heavy breast, he went with her into his tiny bedroom.

*　　*　　*

"What's the time?"

Her voice sounded lazy and sleepy.

Johnny lifted his wrist. It was a few minutes after 15.00. She lay naked, her body on his, her blonde head half on his shoulder and half on the pillow.

"Just after three."

"Oh, damn! I must go to the village." She swung off him and on to her feet, standing, looking down at him.

He looked up, feasting his eyes on her suntanned body. He reached up to touch her, but she moved out of his reach.

"Do you want to come with me?"

He very nearly said he would, then he remembered it would be safer to keep out of sight, to keep away from the village.

"I guess I'll stay. What have you got to go for?"

"The mail if any and the newspaper. Ed likes the newspaper."

"Anything I can do while you're away?"

"You've done enough." She smiled down at him. "You're not much to look at but you know how to satisfy a woman."

"Good?"

"Hmmm."

She went away and reaching for a cigarette Johnny lit up, then relaxed on the bed.

She had been good too, he thought: starving for it. He lay there, thinking about her for the next half hour, then getting off the bed, he took a swim.

He was dressed and sitting on the deck when she returned in the motorboat. The time now was 16.30. He helped her scramble up on deck, then tied up the boat.

"Want to see the paper?" She offered it to him. "I'll stuff the bass," and she left him.

Newspapers seldom interested Johnny except to read the sports news. He glanced at the headlines, found nothing to hold his attention, turned to page two, paused to read an account of a girl who had been found raped and murdered, grimaced, then flicked through the rest of the pages until he came to the funnies. He read "Peanuts" and grinned, then as he was turning to the sports page a headline caught his eyes.

HAVE YOU SEEN THIS MAN?
$10,000 Reward

Then with a sudden cold sick feeling he saw his own photograph.

With shaking hands he read the letterpress.

Dyson & Dyson! Carlo Tanza's attorneys!

Had Freda seen this? He decided by the way the newspaper was folded when she handed it to him she hadn't opened it.

With sweat beads on his face, he studied the photograph. It had been taken some twenty years ago: a prison shot and yet there was a likeness. His hand went to his beard. No! No one could recognize him from this photograph!

Known to favour a St Christopher medal.

The cunning bastards!

She had seen the medal!

He looked furtively over his shoulder, his heart thumping. She wanted money! Ten thousand dollars would be more than tempting! All she had to do was to get over to the village and call Dyson & Dyson. They would be in his lap within twenty-four hours and that would be his end!

What to do?

His first reaction was to destroy the newspaper, but that wouldn't help. He knew enough of Tanza's thoroughness to be sure the ad would run a week ... even longer. Sooner or later, either Scott or Freda would see it.

Get out fast?

He was miles from any place. If he left it would have to be in the dark. It must be a good ten miles down to the freeway and in the dark, he could get hopelessly lost.

Could he trust her? Could he trust anyone?

"Who's offering ten thousand dollars?"

She had come up silently behind him and was leaning over his shoulder. He sat rigid, wanting to crumple the newspaper and throw it in the lake, but fear paralysed him. He watched her hand take the paper from his grasp.

"Ten thousand dollars! Could I use money like that!" She came around and sat by his side.

He watched her read the letterpress and he knew at once when she came to the fatal line: *Known to favour a St Christopher medal.* He saw her stiffen, stare at the photograph, then look at him.

"Is this you?" she asked and tapped the photograph. Johnny hesitated, then he said huskily, "Yes."

"Have you lost your memory?"

He shook his head.

"Who are these people ... Dyson & Dyson?"

His tongue touched his dry lips.

"Mafia people," he said, watching her.

Her eyes widened.

"Mafia?"

"That's right."

She put down the paper.

"I don't understand," and he could see she was shaken, but not so shaken that it curtailed her curiosity.

"You don't want to understand."

"Are you a mafioso?"

"No."

"Then why are they offering all this money?"

"They want to find me and kill me," Johnny said quietly. She flinched.

"Kill you? Why?"

"I did something bad to them."

135

She stared at him for several moments, then she tore the page containing the advert from the paper and offered it to him.

"You'd better burn this, hadn't you? Ten thousand is a lot of money. If Ed sees it he could be tempted: it only means a telephone call, doesn't it?"

"You mean you wouldn't be tempted?"

"Do you think I would?"

He shrugged helplessly.

"As you said, it's a lot of money. You want money. I don't know."

She got to her feet.

"I'm going for a swim."

"Wait ... I want you to understand. I ..."

She had pulled off her shirt, struggled out of her stretch pants and panties and dived into the lake.

Johnny set fire to the sheet of newspaper, then tossed it still burning into the water. He found he was shaking. He sat there, staring at her bobbing head, watching her swim further and further away. Could he trust her? In the night, might she not start thinking of what that money could mean to her? *It only means a telephone call, doesn't it?* She would go across the lake to the village tomorrow. He wouldn't know if she had telephoned or not until Toni, Ernie and the rest of the mob arrived. He wiped the sweat off his face. He had better get out: pack now and clear out. Yet he didn't move. It dawned on him that this woman meant more to him than any woman he had ever met.

Suppose he decided to trust her? Suppose he stayed on? What about Scott? Sooner or later he would see the advert, but he knew nothing about the medal. It was the medal that alerted Freda. He was sure of that. It was the medal that had given him away. Why should Scott connect him with the advert? The photo was taken twenty years ago.

With shaking fingers he undid the chain around his neck and stared at the medal, lying in his palm.

As long as you wear this, nothing really bad can happen to you.

He thought of his mother: a poor, ignorant, superstitious peasant! Goddamn it! Twice the medal had landed him in real trouble! If it hadn't been for the medal he wouldn't now be in hiding. If it hadn't been for the medal Freda wouldn't have guessed who he was.

He stood up.

Away in the distance he could see Freda swimming. The sun was beginning to sink behind the pines.

Lifting his hand, he threw the medal and chain with all his strength into the gathering dusk.

He watched the tiny splash as the medal hit the water.

It was done! It couldn't betray him again!

*　　*　　*

He was sitting on the deck when she came out of the lake, water streaming off her golden body. She picked up her clothes and walked past him into the living-room.

The sun made a red rim around the pines. In another hour, Scott would be back.

During the time she had been swimming, Johnny had thought about her. He had come to the conclusion that this was his woman. He had never had this feeling before. He told himself he was crazy. What did he know about her except there was something in those blue eyes that told him he could trust her.

You mean you wouldn't be tempted?

Do you think I would?

And that look, surprise, then the hurt showed and she had thrown off her clothes and had swum away from him.

That wasn't the action of treachery. Surely, if she planned to betray him, she wouldn't have behaved like that.

Then she was beside him, dressed and sitting down. She looked seriously at him.

"I think we'd better talk, Johnny," she said. "Do you think, by staying here, Ed and I will be in danger?"

He hesitated, then nodded.

"Yes." He paused, then went on. "I'll get Ed to drive me to Richville tomorrow and forget about me. It's the best way."

"I don't want to forget you. I'm in love with you," and she put her hand on his.

He felt a surge of emotion go through him. Many women had told him they loved him. Melanie had, often enough, but none of them had said it the way this woman said it.

"That makes two of us, but I'd better go."

"Could we talk about it?" The slim fingers fondled his wrist. "Could you explain?"

The caressing fingers lulled his caution.

Speaking quietly, staring across the dark waters of the lake, he told her the story of his life. He told her of his yearning to own a boat, about Massino, how Massino had cheated him. He told her about the Big Take, but he didn't tell her how much money was involved.

"I have the money stashed away in East City. If it wasn't for the medal there would have been no problem. I could have stayed there. Massino wouldn't have suspected me. Then later, I would have taken the money and ducked out."

"Is there much money?" she asked.

He looked at her. Her face was expressionless and she wasn't looking at him.

"Enough."

"If you got the money would you take me away from here?"

"Yes."

"Would you choose between me and your boat? Would you give up your boat to keep me?"

He didn't hesitate.

"No. You either go with the boat or I'll stake you and we part. I'm risking my life for the boat: it's that important to me."

She nodded.

"I'm glad. I said it before and I'll say it again: you're all man. I'll come with you and I'll help on the boat."

"If they find me here, they could kill you."

"If I'm going to share this money with you, Johnny, I must share the risk ... that's fair, isn't it?"

"Think about it. Let's talk about it tomorrow. I've still got to get the money."

"Where have you hidden it?"

He smiled at her.

"Where they won't think of looking for it."

"Isn't it dangerous to go back for it?"

"Yes ... it's a hell of a risk."

"But I could get it, couldn't I? They don't know me."

A tiny red light of warning lit up in Johnny's mind. Suppose he told her where the money was? Suppose he gave her the locker key? She could hire a car and drive to East City, take the two bags, load them into the car and that would be the last time he would ever see her. How can anyone trust anyone when there was so much money involved? She said she loved him: she had said it in such a way that he believed her, but when she dragged those two heavy bags out of the locker might she not be tempted to betray him?

He remembered what she had said: *You're not much to look at.* He wasn't. He was fourteen years older than she. With all that money, with her looks, she could make a wonderful life for herself without having a short, heavily-built man of forty-two in her hair.

The sound of the approaching truck saved him from answering.

"Here's Ed. We'll talk tomorrow."

"Yes."

She got up and went hastily into the kitchen.

Scott had his swim, admired the bass Johnny had caught, then came out on deck, joining Johnny while Freda cooked the dinner.

"Had a good day?" Scott asked, lighting a cigarette. He looked slyly at Johnny.

"Fine. And you?"

"The usual." Scott flicked ash into the lake. "Did she give out?"

Johnny stiffened.

"Come again?"

"Did you lay her?"

"Look, Ed, cut that talk out! I don't like it. She's your wife! Haven't you any respect for her?"

Scott gave a sneering laugh.

"I told you I couldn't care less. I was just curious to know if you made it."

"Like I said ... cut it out!"

Scott eyed him.

"Maybe you like it fancy. I do. If ever you want something fancy come to Richville with me. I know a couple of chicks ..."

"I'm a lot older than you, Ed. You look after your sex life and I'll look after mine. Okay?"

Scott studied him, then shrugged.

"Yeah. I guess when I get as old as you, it won't be a problem." He gave a sly grin. "I bet Freda's disappointed. I get the idea she's itching for it."

"Then why don't you give it to her?" Johnny tried to soften his voice, but his anger showed.

"She's not my style."

Johnny suddenly hated this man as he had seldom hated any man. He got to his feet as Freda came on to the deck.

"You can eat," she said.

It was while they were finishing the bass that Scott said, "You got a younger brother, Johnny?"

Johnny became instantly alert. He paused to finish the last morsel of fish on his plate, then shook his head.

"I've no relations."

"Just an idea." Scott pushed aside his plate. "There's an odd ad in the *Richville Times*. I have it here." He shoved back his chair and crossing to where he had left his jacket, he took out a folded newspaper.

Johnny and Freda exchanged quick glances as Scott put the paper in front of Johnny.

"What do you think of that ... ten thousand dollars!"

Johnny pretended to read the letterpress, shrugged and reached for a cigarette.

"Funny thing," Scott went on. "I looked up suddenly just now and you seem to resemble this photograph. I wondered if it could be a young brother."

"Never had a brother," Johnny said.

Scott passed the newspaper to Freda.

"Don't you think this guy looks like Johnny?"

Freda glanced at the photograph.

"Maybe." Her voice was casual. "You can't say Johnny is exactly an oil painting, can you?" and getting up, she began to collect the plates. Johnny helped her while Scott continued to stare at the photograph.

Out in the kitchen, Freda washed up while Johnny dried. They didn't speak, but both were aware of tension.

Returning to the living-room, they found Scott still staring at the ad. Freda went out on deck and as Johnny followed her, Scott said, "Funny sort of ad, isn't it?"

Johnny paused and came back to the table. He sat down.

"It sure is."

"What do you imagine the idea is offering all this money for a guy who's lost his memory?"

"Rich parents, I guess ... anxious to find him."

Scott studied the photograph.

"Doesn't look as if he comes from rich parents, does he?" He glanced at Johnny. "Bit on the rough side ... like you and me."

"Yeah."

"Ten thousand dollars! If I had all that money I'd buy me three more trucks and I'd really be in the business." Scott's face lit up. "Finding drivers is easy, but getting capital for trucks is something else."

"Ever thought of doubling your turn-over without buying more trucks?" Johnny asked, anxious to get Scott's mind off the ad.

"How?"

"You deliver crates of shrimps to Richville ... right?"

"So?"

"But you come back empty. Can't you get freight from Richville to bring back to New Symara?"

"Do you imagine I haven't thought of that?" Scott said scornfully. "You go out and sniff the truck. It stinks of shrimps. No one wants haulage that stinks that bad. I've tried, and anyway, there's nothing in Richville that New Symara wants."

"Just an idea." Johnny got to his feet. "I guess I'll turn in. See you."

Scott nodded.

Johnny left him still staring at the ad.

* * *

Lying in his little bed, watching the moon while he thought, Johnny wasn't ready for sleep. He thought of Freda. Suppose he could trust her? She would be safe going to the Greyhound bus station and getting the money. But could he trust her? Then his mind switched to Scott. Had he convinced him that he had no connection with the ad?

He closed his eyes, trying to force himself to sleep. Then he became alert. He heard Freda enter her room. What a woman! His mind dwelt on the three times they had made love and he had the urge to leave his bed and go into her room and take her again.

Then a slight sound made him stiffen. His door was gently opening. He lay still, his hand reaching under his pillow for his gun.

The moonlight coming through the open window shone directly on the door and through half closed eyes he saw Scott was looking at him through the half-open door.

Johnny emitted a soft snore, watching Scott who stood there, still, listening. Johnny snored again and the door closed silently.

What did this mean? He asked himself, now fully awake. He listened. He heard Freda's door open.

"Come out on deck." Scott's whisper came clearly to Johnny. "Don't say anything ... he's asleep."

Johnny waited. He heard soft movements, then silence. He slid out of his bed, opened his door and peered into the moon-lit living-room. He saw Scott and Freda through the window. They were on the deck. Moving like a ghost, he crept into the living-room as he heard Scott say, "Look at this."

He had a flashlight in his hand and he was directing the beam on to a sheet of newsprint. Johnny knew at once it was the ad. He moved further forward.

"See?" Scott said, his voice low and excited. "I've pencilled a beard on him. It's Johnny!"

"What are you talking about?" Freda's voice was also a whisper but it came clearly to Johnny. "This man's twenty years younger."

"Could be an old photograph."

They were standing side by side by the deck rail. Scott was wearing pyjamas. Freda had a shortie nightdress. Johnny could see her long legs through the moonlit flimsy material.

"Sit down. I want to talk to you."

Johnny watched them move to the bamboo chairs and sit, side by side. He moved forward so he now stood in the darkness within three feet of them, listening through the open window behind them.

"I've been thinking about this," Scott said. "This missing man is Johnny Bianda. Our lodger calls himself Johnny Bianco. For all we know he has lost his memory and imagines he's Bianco and not Bianda. The more I look at this photo, now I've put on the beard, the surer I am this is the man they want. Ten thousand dollars! Imagine! What do you think?"

Johnny held his breath. What she would say must tell him if he could trust her or not.

"He doesn't act like a man who's lost his memory." Freda's voice was calm. "We were talking this afternoon. He was telling me about his rent-collection experiences. No ... you're pipe dreaming."

"Suppose I call these people: Dyson & Dyson? Where's the harm? They can send someone to take a look at him. They will probably have dozens of people telephoning so what have we to lose? We might hit the jackpot."

"And if we do ... what happens?"

"Ten thousand dollars! You want to leave me, don't you? You've had enough of this, haven't you?"

"Yes."

"Fine. So I give you two thousand and with the rest I buy three more trucks and I'm in business. Tomorrow, I'll call these people from Richville. If we're unlucky, it's too bad, but if we aren't ..."

Johnny's heart now was thumping so hard he was scared they would hear.

"Let's make sure," Freda said. "I'll send him out fishing tomorrow and while he's on the lake, I'll go through his things. This thing about a St Christopher medal. He might have one. If I find it, we'll know for sure it's him."

"What's wrong with me telephoning tomorrow? They can but look at him."

A pause, then she said, "Can't you use your brains? If we are really sure we can ask for more ... we could ask for fifteen thousand: Five for me and ten for you."

"I hadn't thought of that. Yeah ... but you don't get five, baby. You'll get four."

"So all right. I get four."

Scott stood up.

"You check his things. Imagine! Fifteen thousand dollars!"

Johnny moved silently back to his bedroom, closed the door and lay on the bed.

So he could trust her! She was clever! She had gained a day ... but what then?

There was no sleep for him that night.

*   *   *

Carlo Tanza came into Massino's office, kicked the door shut and dumped his heavy body into a chair.

"We've certainly started something with that ad!" he exclaimed. "Already it has produced three hundred and forty-nine telephone calls. Dyson is flipping his lid. Every call has to be checked out."

Massino glared at him.

"It was your bright idea."

"It was a good idea, but how was I to know so many bastards resemble this bastard? So, okay, we're checking them out but it's going to take time."

"That's your business," Massino said. "I pay ... you produce. One thing I do know, if the money is in one of those lockers across the street, the sonofabitch will never get it ... that's something I'm damn well certain about!"

8

The sound of the truck had scarcely died away when Johnny's bedroom door opened and Freda came in.

In the grey light of the dawn, she looked to Johnny the most desirable woman in the world, but this was no time for love.

She sat on the side of his bed.

"He talked to me last night," she said.

"I know. I heard every word," Johnny said and put his hand on hers. "You played it smart, but when he comes back tonight ... what's going to happen?"

"I'll tell him I'm sure you're not the man he thinks you are. I'll tell him I've seen your driving licence and it's in the name of Bianco. I'll say there's no St Christopher medal."

Johnny shook his head.

"That won't stop him. He's money hungry. As he said; what's there to lose except the price of a telephone call?"

"Then let's get out of here," Freda said. "Let's get the money and get lost. I know where I can hire a car in the village. We'll drive to East City, pick up the money, then head north? What do you say?"

He lay back on his pillow and marvelled at her ignorance of the net that was closing around him.

"If only it could be as simple as that," he said.

"But they don't know me!" Freda said impatiently. "Where have you hidden the money? Why can't I get it while you wait, out of sight?"

"East City is swarming with Massino's Men. Every one of them will have a description of the bags, holding the money. Two shabby red hold-alls with black leather handles," Johnny said. "Anyone seen carrying two such bags wouldn't survive five minutes."

"Then we'll buy a trunk and put the two bags in the trunk ... what's the matter with that?"

Johnny now felt he had to tell her everything.

"The bags are in a left-luggage locker in the Greyhound bus station, right opposite Massino's office. You couldn't load them into a trunk without being seen."

"But there must be some way I could get them!"

"Massino's sharp. Maybe he has thought of the lockers. Maybe he has them staked out. Before we do anything, I've got to check." Johnny thought for a moment. "Where's the nearest call booth?"

"In the village ... the local store."

"I've a contact in East City. He'll tell me what's happening. How soon does the store open?"

"Seven-thirty."

He looked at his watch. The time was 05.30.

"Will you take me across in the boat?"

She hesitated.

"They're all eyes and ears over there. So far, they don't know you exist. You could cause a sensation."

"I've got to get to a phone."

She thought for a long moment.

"Suppose I tell Salvadore you're my stepbrother on a visit? Be nice to him. He's easy to con: you just have to be nice to him."

"An Italian?" Johnny stiffened. "Who's he?"

"He owns the store: Salvadore Bruno. He's harmless. If we time our arrival as the store opens, no one will be around. You really mean you must phone?"

"Yes."

"You mean once you know it will be all right, we can hire a car and get the money?"

"I've got to know first."

She nodded.

"I'll get coffee. There's time."

He reached out and pulled her down on him.

"There's also time for coffee."

* * *

The motorboat drifted into the little harbour. Johnny could see the store: a low, ramshackle building, facing the waterfront. He glanced at his watch. It was a minute after 07.30 and he saw the door leading into the store, was standing open.

He was wearing his bush jacket to conceal his gun and holster. His eyes darted along the waterfront, but there was no sign of life.

Freda jumped onto the quay. Johnny tossed the rope to her and she secured the boat.

Together they crossed the dirt road and walked into the store.

"The phone's there," Freda said and pointed.

As Johnny stepped into the call booth, he saw a short, fat man come out from behind a curtain. He shut the door, then turned his back and inserted coins. He called Sammy's apartment.

There was a delay, then Sammy's sleepy voice came over the line.

"Who's this?"

"Sammy! Wake up! This is Johnny!"

"Who?"

"Johnny!"

A low moan of fear came over the line.

"Listen, Sammy ... what's happening up there? What's the news?"

"Mr Johnny ... I asked you ... I begged you not to contact me. I could get into real trouble. I ..."

"Cut it out, Sammy! You're my friend ... remember? What's happening?"

"I don't know. I don't know nothin'. No one talks any more, Mr Johnny. I swear. I don't know nothin'!"

"I want you to do something for me, Sammy."

"Me? Haven't I done enough, Mr Johnny? You've got all my money. Cloe keeps worrying me for money and I've got none now to give her. My brother ..."

"Skip it, Sammy! I told you: you'll get your money back. Now listen carefully. You know the Greyhound bus station?"

"Yeah. I know it."

"When you have driven the boss to his office, go in there and buy a newspaper. Wander around. I want to know if any of the mob are staked out there. You getting this, Sammy?"

"They *are* staked out there, Mr Johnny. Don't ask me why, but they are. I went in there last night to get cigarettes and Toni and Ernie were hanging around."

Johnny nodded to himself. So Massino suspected the money was in one of those lockers.

"Okay, Sammy. Now don't worry about your money. I'll send it to you soon," and he hung up.

For a long moment, Johnny stood staring at the coin box. It was a matter of patience. For how long would Massino have the lockers watched? He could not know the money was there: he was guessing. This had to be thought about. How to deal with Scott tonight?

He pushed open the booth door and moved into the store. "Johnny! Come and meet Salvadore," Freda called. She was standing by one of the counters. On the other side was the short, fat man who thrust out his hand.

"Glad to meet you," he said with a wide smile. "Big surprise. Mrs Freda never told me she had a half-brother. Welcome to Little Creek."

As Johnny shook hands, he took this man in with a quick searching glance: balding, around sixty, a bushy moustache, small, intelligent eyes and a stubbly chin.

"Passing through," he said. "Got business in Miami. Nice store you have here."

"Yeah, yeah, it's all right." The little eyes dwelt on Johnny's face. "You Italian like me?"

"My mother was Italian," Johnny said. "Our old man was a Swede." He looked at Freda who nodded.

"Mother comes out in you, huh?"

"You can say that."

"Yeah." A pause. "You staying long?"

"It's pretty nice up here. I'm in no hurry to get to work." Johnny forced a laugh. "I heard a lot about this place when Freda wrote, but I had no idea it's as good as this."

"You fish?"

"I like it. Yesterday, I landed a four-pounder first try ... a bass."

Salvadore beamed.

"So you're a fisherman."

"Could I have two pounds of bacon and a dozen eggs," Freda broke in.

"In a moment."

Salvadore hurried to another counter. Johnny and Freda exchanged glances. They didn't say anything.

Ten minutes later, after more talk, they walked across the quay to the boat.

Salvadore watched them go. The benign expression on his fat face slowly faded and his little eyes became like marbles.

He reached under the counter and produced yesterday's *Florida Times*. Quickly, he thumbed through the pages until he came to the Have You Seen This Man? advertisement. He stared for several moments at the photograph, then taking a pencil from behind his ear, he carefully pencilled in a beard. After staring at the photograph again, he crossed to the call booth, inserted a coin and dialled a number.

A growling voice replied.

"Bruno. Little Creek," Salvadore said. "This guy Johnny Bianda. There's a guy just arrived, calling himself Johnny who looks like him."

"What guy?"

Salvadore talked.

"If she says he's her half-brother why the hell can't he be her half-brother."

"This doll isn't getting it from her husband. It's my bet she'd say anything to get it and it's my bet this guy is giving it to her."

"Okay. I'll send someone to take a look. We've got hundreds of goddamn suspects to check out, but I'll send someone."

"When?"

"How do I know? When I've got a man free."

"If it's him, I get the reward?"

"If it's him," and the line went dead.

* * *

The noise of the outboard engine made conversation impossible. Johnny sat in the prow of the boat, his mind active. The store-keeper had alerted his sense of danger. He had had to phone Sammy, but now he realized the risk he had taken. There were Mafiosi everywhere. So they were watching the lockers at the Greyhound bus station! As he sat in the prow of the boat, feeling the breeze against his face, watching the prow cut through the still waters, he felt the net closing in on him.

When he had tied up and had followed Freda on to the deck of the houseboat, he dropped into one of the bamboo chairs.

"Well?"

She stood over him and he looked up into her bright blue eyes.

"They're watching the lockers."

The disappointment in her eyes made him uneasy. She was so money hungry, he thought. She sat by his side.

"So what do we do?"

"That's right ... so what do we do?" He thought, staring across the lake. "When I planned this steal, baby, I told myself I would have to be patient. I told myself it wouldn't be safe spending that money for a couple of years."

She stiffened.

"Two years?"

"As long as the money stays in the locker, it's safe. Try and move it and you and me are dead and the money goes

153

back to Massino. Sooner or later, he'll get tired of watching the lockers. It might take a month ... even six months, but I have my contact in East City. He'll tell me when the heat's off and until it's off, we have to wait.

"You're not planning to stay here six months, are you?"

"No ... I've got to find myself a job. I'm handy with boats. I'll go to Tampa ... I'll find something there."

"And what about me?" The hard note in her voice made him look at her. She was staring at him, her eyes glittering.

"I've some money. It'll be rough like this, but if you want to come, I'd like to have you with me."

"How much money did you take from this man, Johnny? You haven't told me."

And he wasn't going to tell her.

"Around fifty thousand," he said.

"You're risking your life for fifty thousand?"

"That's it. I want to own a boat. I can get one for that money."

She stared at him and he saw she didn't believe him.

"It's more than that, isn't it? You don't trust me."

"I don't know. I never got around to counting it. My guess is fifty, but it could be more ... could be less."

She sat still, thinking.

He watched her, then said quietly. "You're wondering if ten thousand in the hand is better than fifty thousand in the bush, aren't you?"

She stiffened, then shook her head.

"No. I'm trying to imagine myself on a boat," but he knew she was lying.

"Don't do anything you'll regret," he said. "Look, suppose when you go over for the mail you call these attorneys. Let me tell you what will happen. Five or six men will arrive. They'll try to take me alive, because dead, they will never find the money. One thing I'm sure about: no one takes me alive. I've seen what happens to men who have tried to double cross Massino. He has them tied to chairs and beats them with a baseball bat: careful not to kill them, breaking their bones and then he finally sticks a butcher's hook in their throats and hangs them in the chair until they die: so no one is taking me alive. So there will be a gun battle and during the gun battle you'll stop a bullet. Believe me, baby, no one will live to collect that ten thousand dollar reward: that's just bait. So don't do anything you'll regret."

She shivered, then put her hand on his.

"I wouldn't betray you, Johnny. I swear I wouldn't, but what about Ed?"

"Yeah, I've been thinking about him. Here's what you tell him. You tried to get into my suitcase while I was fishing, but it was locked. So when I got back, you went over to collect the mail and the newspaper. You telephoned these attorneys and said you thought the man they were looking for was in Little Creek. And what do you imagine they said?" Johnny looked at her. "They said the man had been found in Miami and they thanked you for calling them and they were sorry you had been troubled. How will Ed react to that?"

She relaxed.

"That's smart. He won't want to spend more money on a long distance. Yes, he'll drop it."

"That's the way I figured it. I can stay here until the end of the week, then I'll tell him I'm moving on. We'll hire that car you talked about and we'll go to Tampa."

"Why wait? Why not go tomorrow?"

"That's not the way to play it. During the next five days, you're going to fall in love with me and you'll leave him a letter telling him so and that you and me are going off together. Rush it and he'll get suspicious. He might even phone these attorneys. He might ask at the village and find out what car we've hired. Then we wouldn't get far, baby. Believe me, this is a game of patience."

"Wait! That's all I do! Wait!" Freda got to her feet. "God! I'm sick of this life!"

"It's better to be sick of life than not have a life." Johnny stood up. "I'll go get some supper."

He left her and went to his room. Closing the door, he slid the bolt. Then taking out a spare khaki shirt, he felt in the breast pocket. From it he took the key to the left-luggage locker. He looked at it for a brief moment. Engraved on it was the number of the locker: 176: the key to $186,000!

Sitting on the bed, he untied his shoe lace, put the key into his shoe and then tightened the lace. It wasn't comfortable, but it was safe!

A few minutes later he returned to the deck.

Freda was in the living-room, using the vacuum cleaner.

"I'll be back," he called, then went to the boat, started the engine and headed out to the middle of the lake.

*　　*　　*

The telephone bell rang just as Massino was about to leave his office for home.

"Get it!" he barked to Lu Berilli who scooped up the receiver.

"It's Mr Tanza," he said and offered the receiver.

Cursing, Massino snatched the receiver from him, sat on the corner of his desk and said, "What is it, Carlo? I'm just going home."

"Just had a hot tip come in," Carlo said. "Could be nothing, but could be something. A man, answering to Bianda's description is living in a houseboat near Little Creek: that's five miles from New Symara. He's been there about two days and living with a man and his wife. The woman has hot pants. The husband is a trucker and away all day. She's Swedish and says this guy is her half-brother. He's as Italian as we are. This is a straight tip and the source is reliable."

"So why bother me?" Massino demanded. "You're looking for him, aren't you? Well, check this punk out."

"We want one of your boys to identify him. No point in starting anything without being sure. Can you send someone?"

"Okay. I'll send Toni."

"Fine. Tell him to fly to New Symara and then take a taxi to the Waterfront Bar. All the taxi drivers know it. He's to ask for Luigi. He's our contact man. He'll fix it. Toni has three or four men who'll take him to Little Creek. Okay?"

Massino scribbled on a pad.

"Yeah," he said and hung up.

He turned to Berilli.

"Find Toni. Give him this. He's to fly on the first flight out. Tell him his job is to identify some guy Tanza thinks is Bianda. Get going!"

Berilli found Toni drinking beer with Ernie in a bar all Massino's men frequented. Toni and Ernie had just come off a long, boring stint of watching the left-luggage lockers and Toni was griping.

Ernie, who never minded a job where he could sit and do nothing, was listening with a bored expression on his fat face.

"Look who's here," he said when he saw Berilli come in.

"That creep!" Toni sneered. "What's he good for?"

Berilli came over and sat at their table.

"You have yourself a job." He hated Toni and it pleased him to be the conveyor of bad news. "The boss says you're to fly right away to New Symara ... wherever the hell that is. Here ... it's all written down."

Toni took the scrap of paper, read it and then looked blankly at Berilli.

"What the hell's this all about?" he demanded.

"This guy Luigi says they think they've spotted Johnny. They want someone to go down there and identify him before they move in."

"Johnny?"

Toni lost colour.

"Yeah. The boss says for you to take off right away."

"That'll be the time," Ernie said and chortled. "When you face Johnny. Man! Would I like to be a long distance witness!"

Toni cursed him.

"You're sure the boss picked me?"

Berilli sneered at him.

"You call him. Don't you want the job?"

Toni licked his lips, aware the two men were watching him and grinning. He got to his feet and left the bar.

*   *   *

Johnny got back to the houseboat around midday with three fair-sized Black Crappie. He had been uncomfortable wearing his bush jacket but he had to wear it to hide his gun and holster. From now on, he told himself, he wouldn't move without his gun. His instinct for danger was alert. While fishing, he had thought of Salvadore. The fat man had been friendly, but that didn't mean a thing. Everywhere there was a Mafia contact. He remembered Salvadore saying: *You Italian like me?* On the face of it a harmless remark, but it could also point to trouble.

All the same the peace of the lake, the quietness, the fact no one came near, although he could see distant boats, gave him a feeling of security, but he would carry his gun.

He dumped the fish into the kitchen sink. There was no sign of Freda. He went into his room, then kneeling, he looked under the bed and he smiled.

He had placed the suitcase at a slight angle and now it was straight. That could only mean Freda had touched it. He pulled it out and examined the locks. They were flimsy enough and it was possible she had a key that could open them. He unlocked the case and counted the ten dollar bills. Of Sammy's money, he had left $2,857. He relocked the case and pushed it under the bed, then he went up on deck.

He sat in the sun for more than an hour, then he heard Freda crossing the creaky jetty.

"Hi! Where have you been?" he asked as she came around the deck and joined him.

"A walk. Did you get any fish?"

"Three Black Crappie."

"God! Crappie again!"

"The bass were shy."

She went to the rail and stood against it, her hands on the rail, her body slightly bent forward. Johnny eyed the soft sweep of her buttocks. He came up behind her, his hands cupping her breasts, his body against her softness.

She slid away from him.

"Skip it!" she said, her voice hard. "We can't spend all the week ------" She used the ugly four letter word and it shocked Johnny.

159

"Take it easy," he said. "This is a game of patience."

"I'll fix the fish." He had a definite feeling that she was now hostile. "Eggs and bacon for lunch."

"Fine."

He watched her walk into the kitchen. This woman could be tricky. He thought of Melanie: no trickiness there. He sat for a long moment, his mind active. Freda must learn he was the boss. If she didn't recognize this fact, he could be in danger.

Getting to his feet, he walked into the kitchen. Freda was washing the fish and she glanced over her shoulder.

"What do you want?"

"Dry your hands."

"I'm busy ... go sit in the sun."

He jerked her around and slapped her face. He was careful not to hit her too hard, but the slap was hard enough to jerk her head back. Her blue eyes blazed and her hand dropped on a kitchen knife by the fish.

He caught her wrist, squeezed and the knife dropped to the floor, then he caught hold of her, pinning her arms to her sides and shoving her out of the kitchen, he forced her along the passage to his room.

"Let me go!" she exclaimed.

She was strong and hard to hold but he handled her. He got her into his room, kicked the door shut, then released her.

"Get them off or I'll rip them off!" he said.

"Who do you imagine you are?" Her eyes were blazing with fury. "You'll have me when I want you and not before! Now get out!"

To Johnny who in the past had been in many brawls, she was pathetically easy. He weaved as she struck at him, her clawed fingers hopelessly out of range. Then he had her on her back on the bed. Her wrists now gripped in his hand.

"Going to behave, baby, or do I really get rough?"

She stared up at him, then relaxed.

"I'll behave."

He released her wrists, undid her belt and pulled the stretch pants off her.

Later, she said, "I'm starving." She ran her fingers down his hard back. "I love you. You're all man. Whatever you say, whatever you do is all right with me."

She slid off the bed and went away.

While he dressed, he heard the sizzling sound of bacon cooking. He went into the kitchen. Freda, naked, was cracking eggs into the pan.

He came up behind her and stroked her buttocks.

"Stop it, Johnny, or we don't eat."

While they were eating, Johnny said, "In five days from now, you and me will be on the road together ... starting a new life."

Freda smiled at him.

"I want it! Johnny ... you don't know how much I want it!"

They spent the rest of the afternoon sitting on the deck, soaking up the sun. Around 18.30, Freda said, "I'll start supper. You take a walk. Don't get back for an hour. I must convince Ed."

"I'll take the boat, maybe I'll catch a bass."

"If it's Black Crappie, put it back."

Well away from the houseboat, Johnny sat in the boat and thought of her. He wondered too what Melanie was doing. If she had found someone to replace him. He wondered what Massino was doing. Probably taking his fat, spoilt wife on some shindig. During the hour, he caught four Black Crappie and put them back, then he turned the boat and headed back to the houseboat.

As he got on deck, he saw Scott hosing down his truck. He waved and Scott waved back. He went into the kitchen.

Freda nodded.

"It's all right. There's nothing for us to worry about. He's dropped it."

Johnny drew in a slow deep breath.

"You're sure?"

"I'm sure."

* * *

A little after 11.15 an air-taxi landed at the New Symara airport and from it came Toni Cappelo.

Ten minutes later a taxi dropped him outside the Waterfront Bar. He regarded the outside of the building and was surprised. This joint, he decided, had a lot of style. Situated opposite the yacht basin, the swank district of New Symara, the Waterfront Bar was the haunt of the rich. Tables, shaded by gaily coloured umbrellas, stood before the building which was painted white with sky-blue wooden shutters. There was a red carpet leading into the bar over which was a blue-and-white, barrel-shaped canopy. The tables were crowded with fat, rich-looking people off their yachts.

Toni felt a little shabby as he walked into the bar, carrying his suitcase. He was aware people were staring at him and he now wished his clothes matched theirs.

An Italian in a white jacket and blood-red trousers, intercepted him.

"You want something?" The contempt in the man's voice give Toni a rush of blood to his head.

"Luigi, you punk," he snarled, "and hurry it up!"

The waiter's eyes bulged.

"Signore Moro is busy."

"Tell him Massino," Toni said. "He's expecting me!"

The waiter's contempt went away. He pointed.

"Excuse me. Please go ahead. First door behind the bar."

Toni found Luigi Moro behind a desk as big as a billiard table. He was scribbling figures on a scratch pad and as Toni walked in, he leaned back in his chair and nodded.

Luigi Moro was around sixty-five years of age, enormously fat, his nose slightly flattened – a gift from a tough cop when he had been young – his dark, shifty eyes as animated as the eyes of a dead fish.

"Sit down ... have a cigar." He waved to a chair and pushed a silver box containing Havanas in Toni's direction.

Toni wasn't a cigar smoker. He sat down on the edge of the chair. He had heard about Luigi Moro, one of the Mafia's favourites: a man people had to respect or there was trouble.

Moro lit a cigar, taking his time, looking thoughtfully at Toni.

"I've heard about you: you're good with a gun."

Toni nodded.

"How's Joe?"

"He's okay."

"A big steal." Moro laughed. "I bet he's flipping his lid."

Toni didn't say anything.

"We got this tip," Moro said. "We've got over a hundred tips but this one looks good. I've got all my men out checking other tips so suppose you go out to Little Creek and take a gander? It could be negative and I don't want to pull my boys off the work they're doing. You take a gander and if it's straight up, call me and we'll go out there and get him."

Toni felt a chill go up his spine.

"Don't you send anyone with me?"

Moro stared at him.

"I told you ... the boys are busy." He flicked ash into the big, silver ashtray on his desk. "You're Massino's top gunman, aren't you?"

"Yeah."

"Fine. You can handle this." He pressed a button on his desk and a minute or so later the door opened and a young long-haired Italian came in. "Take this guy to Little Creek, Leo, wise him up. Introduce him to Salvadore. Tell the old buzzard my compliments."

The young man stared at Toni, then jerked his head to the door. Toni followed him out into the passage, hating him: a possible homo: very lean, white-faced, glittering eyes, could be on pot.

In silence they walked out of the building by the back exit to a shabby Lincoln.

Leo slid under the wheel and Toni got in the passenger's seat.

Leo turned and stared at Toni.

"I heard about you ... a trigger man." He grinned, showing good white teeth. "Rather you than me."

"Get going," Toni snarled. "Rest the lip."

"Tough too?" Leo laughed. "You watch the telly?"

"Get moving!"

Leo opened the glove compartment and dropped a pair of powerful field glasses in Toni's lap.

"They're for you."

Thirty minutes, later, they pulled up outside Salvadore Bruno's store.

"This is where I kiss you off," Leo said. "Have a ball. If it's him, call us. Okay?"

The time now was 11.45. There was some activity on the waterfront. As Toni got out of the car he was aware people were looking curiously at him. He slung the field glasses by their strap on his shoulder and walked into the store as Leo drove away.

Salvadore was busy serving customers. When he saw Toni, he called and his fat wife appeared to take over.

Salvadore beckoned to Toni who followed him behind the curtain and into Salvadore's living-room.

"You from Luigi?"

"Yeah."

Salvadore opened a drawer in the table and took out a large scale map.

"Here's where we are: here's where he is," he said, pointing with a pencil. "You can take my boat or you can take my car and drive around the lake."

Toni blotted sweat off his face with his sleeve.

"Maybe the boat is better."

He didn't want to get too close to Johnny if this suspect was Johnny.

"Yes. There are always fishermen on the lake." Salvadore eyed the field glasses. "With those you can see without being seen. I'll loan you a fishing rod. Just go out on the lake and act you're fishing ... okay?"

"Yeah."

A pause, then Salvadore said, "If it's him, I get the reward ... yes?"

"How the hell do I know?" Toni snarled. "Why the hell should I care anyway?"

"That's no way to talk to your betters," Salvadore said. "I ask a polite question: I expect a polite answer."

"So get stuffed!" Toni snarled. "How's about something to eat?"

Salvadore moved forward. His hand caught Toni's wrist in a grip of steel, his vast belly, rock hard, smashed into Toni's side, driving the breath out of him. His arm was twisted and he found himself gasping and on his knees. He felt a hard, sweaty hand slap him heavily around his ears, then dazed, he groped for his gun as Salvadore released him.

"Don't do it!"

The snap in Salvadore's voice made him turn and look up. He found himself looking into the menacing barrel of a .45.

"All right, my friend," Salvadore said gently, "so now you'll be polite. I may be fat and old, but I've eaten boys like you for breakfast. So now you ask politely for dinner."

Toni got unsteadily to his feet.

Salvadore put his gun back into its holster, hidden under his thin coat.

"Look," he said and the gun appeared in his hand, then he chuckled. "I was Lucky's best man. I'm still good. Okay, so I'm old, but I've never lost the sharpness," and the gun disappeared. He patted Toni's shoulder. "So you want something to eat, huh?"

"Yes, please and thank you," Toni said huskily. "I guess I could eat something."

Salvadore put his thick arm around Toni's shoulders.

"Come." He led him into the kitchen. "Always in my home there is good food."

An hour later, Toni got into Salvadore's small fishing boat, awkwardly carrying a fishing rod and the field glasses. Salvadore had fitted him out in a dark blue shirt, a pair of Levis and a bush hat. He showed him how to start the outboard engine.

"Just put the rod in here," he said pointing to a clip on the side of the boat. "Don't get too close to the houseboat. If anyone comes up to you ... there are many fishermen on the lake ... tell them you are my friend. They won't bother you."

Toni steered the boat out into the middle of the lake, then cut the engine. He could see, in the distance, the houseboat. He clipped the rod into position, then focused the glasses on the houseboat.

He was startled at the power of the glasses.

The houseboat seemed to spring forward at him as he peered through the eyepieces. He could see the flaked paint, the holes in the deck and the rust on the rails. There was no one to be seen. He sat there, feeling the sun burning his back and settled himself to watch.

9

The previous evening just before Scott had gone to bed, Johnny had asked permission to borrow the 12 bore shotgun.

"Thought I might take a walk in the woods and bag something for supper."

"Sure," Scott said. "A good idea. I never get time now for shooting. You could find coot or pigeon."

So the following morning after a swim, Johnny took the gun with a pocketful of 6 shot cartridges and told Freda he would be back for lunch.

"Don't get lost," she warned him. "Keep to the path and don't go far."

He spent the whole morning in the jungle and enjoyed himself. He bagged four pigeons and two wild duck, and he felt ten feet tall as he walked into the kitchen where Freda was cooking steaks.

"Quite the man around the home," she said as he showed her the birds. "Suppose, this afternoon, you go on making yourself useful? I've asked Ed to put up four shelves over there. If I've asked him once, I've asked him twenty times. The wood's all cut. How about it?"

"Sure," Johnny said. "I'll fix it."

They had lunch, then went to bed together and around 15.00 Freda said she would go across to the village and collect the mail and the newspaper.

"I'll fix the shelves."

It was because he spent the next two hours in the kitchen that Toni, sweltering in the sun, didn't catch a glimpse of him, but he did see Freda as she came on deck, got in the motorboat and headed towards him.

Hastily, Toni hid the field glasses and lifted the rod from its clip.

Freda's boat passed him by a hundred feet and he was aware she looked at him. He kept his head lowered and flicked the rod with what he hoped was a professional movement.

Some chick! he thought. Man! Could he use a piece of tail like her!

If it were really Johnny holed up in the houseboat, Toni thought, he certainly had it good. But was it Johnny? He surveyed the houseboat once again with his glasses, but he saw no sign of life. Hell! He was getting roasted alive out in this goddamn sun and he was aware that there were no other fishermen on the lake. Maybe he had better go back. He could be attracting attention by sitting out in the boat like this. Again he searched the houseboat with his glasses, then still seeing nothing, he laid the rod down and decided to return. He would come out later when the sun was less fierce.

Unused to the sun, he was now getting painfully sunburned. He moved over to the outboard engine, caught hold of the starting handle and yanked. There was a splutter and nothing else. Cursing, he yanked on the cord again. Again no results.

He glared at the engine and cursed it. Four more times he yanked at the starting cord with sweat streaming off him, but the engine wouldn't fire. He sat on the side of the boat, his shirt soaked with sweat.

Salvadore had told him he would have no trouble with the engine. All he had to do was to pull the cord. Now the bastard wouldn't start! He could get burned alive out here!

He had been crazy to have used the boat! He knew nothing about boats, or outboard engines. He couldn't even swim! He looked longingly at the cool water around him.

His gun harness was chafing his skin. He was wearing it under his shirt. He reached inside the shirt, undid the harness and took it off, laying the gun by the fishing rod.

What the hell was he to do?

He went back to the engine and dragged at the cord. The engine spluttered and died.

Then he heard the phut-phut of an approaching motorboat. Looking up, he saw Freda returning from Little Creek. He waved to her and she cut her engine and steering her boat, came drifting up to him.

"Are you in trouble?" she asked.

Toni stared at her. His eyes took in the sweep of her breasts, the firm outline of her buttocks, her blonde hair and her brilliant blue eyes.

"Yeah. She won't start."

"It's the heat. You're oiled up. Take the plug out and clean it. You'll start then."

Toni looked around.

"I've got no tools."

"I'll do it. You hold the boats together."

She opened a locker and took out a tool kit, then slid into his boat. As she got in, her foot caught in the harness of his gun and she stumbled, rocking the boats. He caught hold of her, steadying her and the feel of her arm in his hand sent a sexual jolt through him. He kicked the gun and the harness out of sight under one of the seats.

She was kneeling, her back to him and she opened the tool kit.

"You're new around here, aren't you?" she said as she got out a box spanner.

"Yeah. I'm a friend of Bruno." He eyed her back, feeling lust go through him.

"I thought I hadn't seen you before." She got the plug out. "See? Oil."

She turned, holding the plug.

"Never thought of it," Toni said huskily. "I don't know a thing about boats ... just down here on vacation."

"Salvadore is a good friend of mine." She took a rag from the tool kit and cleaned the plug. "It's always nice to see a new face."

He eyed her, wondering what she meant.

"I guess."

"You won't get any fish at this time," she went on as she put the plug back and tightened it. "In another two hours, but it's too hot now."

"You can say that again ... I'm frying."

"Are you staying with Salvadore?"

"That's right."

She looked at him: her blue eyes inviting.

"Maybe I'll see something of you."

Was she giving him the "come on"? Toni wondered, and again lust stabbed him like a sword thrust.

"Why not?" He peered at her. "Bruno tells me you have your half-brother staying with you."

"He left early this morning. He has business in Miami." She smiled. "I miss his company. It's lonely for me. My husband doesn't get back until late."

"Yeah. I can imagine."

She got into her boat.

"You try now. She'll start." She reached for the starter on her engine. "If you've got nothing to do why not drop by around half-past five?" Her blue eyes met his. "My husband doesn't get back until seven."

Before he could reply, she started her engine, waved to him and sent the boat fast away from him.

Toni stared after her, his heart thumping. If that wasn't an invitation for a lay, what was? And what a lay! But wait, he told himself, suppose Johnny or whoever this punk was hadn't gone? Suppose she was setting him up to walk into a trap? But why should she? He knew her type: a chick with hot pants. Maybe this guy hadn't been her half-brother. Maybe he wasn't Bianda. So he had gone and she had the itch again.

He pulled the starter and the engine fired. With his mind seething with excitement, he headed back to Little Creek.

Salvadore was on the quay and he helped Toni tie up the boat.

"Did you see him?"

"No, but I saw her. The goddamn engine wouldn't start. She fixed it. She says her half-brother left this morning for Miami. She wants me to go over there at half-past five." Toni wiped his sweating face with the back of his hand. "What do you think?"

Salvadore shook his head.

"If he's there you could walk into trouble."

"Yeah, but if he's there why should she ask me over?" He leered. "It's my bet whoever this punk is, he's gone and she wants it. So okay, I go over there, take a look around, slip her what she wants, then tell the boss it wasn't the guy and go back. That makes sense, doesn't it?"

Salvadore looked at him for a long moment.

"It's your funeral. You could be right. Anyway, why should I worry? You can take care of yourself. If you want to go, then go."

"Yeah. How's about a long, cold beer? I'm boiled."

*　　*　　*

Johnny was just putting the last of the shelves in place when he heard the distant sound of Freda's outboard motor. He tightened the final screw and then went to the kitchen window.

He saw her boat coming fast and as he was about to step out on deck, he paused, seeing another boat far out on the lake. His instinct for danger stopped him in his tracks. He watched the other boat with a lone man in it, heading for Little Creek.

Freda steered the boat under the kitchen window and called "Don't come out!" The urgency in her voice told him there was trouble.

He moved into the living-room and waited until she joined him.

"What is it?"

Quickly she told him of her encounter with Toni.

"He has a gun and harness," she concluded. "He says he's Salvadore's friend."

Johnny sat down. He had a feeling of being suffocated. The net was drawing in on him.

"Tell me about him," he said. "What's he look like?"

"Around thirty, thin, dark, good-looking. He had a tattoo on his right arm: a naked woman."

Johnny flinched.

Toni Capello! The tattoo fixed it!

Seeing his reaction, Freda said, "Is he one of them?"

173

"Yes ... he's one of them. They've got close, baby."

They looked at each other and she came to him, kneeling by his side.

"He asked about my half-brother. I said you had gone."

"I must go."

"No!" Her hand touched his face. "We can bluff him, Johnny. I told him to come and see me at five-thirty. I think he'll come. You go out into the jungle and wait. I can convince him you've gone and then they'll look elsewhere, but from now on you stay here and keep out of sight."

He stared at her.

"You asked him to come here?"

"Johnny! I love you! I want you to be safe! He'll come. I'll show him around, then I'll get rid of him. Once he's sure you're not here, he'll go away."

"You don't know what you're doing! This man's dangerous! I know him! You can't have him here alone!"

"There's no man born I can't handle," Freda said and smiled. "I know men. I can handle him. You go into the jungle and wait. I'll get rid of him before Ed gets back."

Johnny stared at her. Then into his mind he remembered what Scott had said: *We swim raw. You don't have to bother about Freda. She's seen more naked men than I've seen shrimps.* He had thought then that this had been a stupid remark from a stupid man, but now he wondered if Scott could have been speaking the truth.

Did it matter? He looked at her. Without her, he could shortly be dead. He felt a moment of sadness, then he shrugged.

"I guess that's the best way to handle it. Okay, I'll go into the jungle, but watch him ... he's as tricky as a snake."

She was watching him.

174

"Don't look like that, Johnny. In another four days, we'll be away from here. I'm doing this for you and only for you."

"Yes." He moved away from her.

For me? he was thinking, or for the money?

"It was smart of me, wasn't it ... to tell him you had gone." He could see she was longing for a little praise, but he couldn't give it. There was a pause, then she went on, "But from now on you must keep out of sight. You must stay indoors, but it's only for four days."

"That's right." He couldn't look at her. He had never felt so depressed. "Watch him. I'll get moving."

"Kiss me."

Did he want to? He forced himself to look at her, then those brilliant blue eyes hooked him. She came into his arms, her fingers going through his hair, her body hard against his.

"Johnny ... Johnny ... I love you," she said, her lips against his cheek. "We'll soon be free of this. Trust me! I'll handle him."

With his gun and vacuum flask of ice water, Johnny went into the hot jungle and sitting in the shade, he settled to wait. From where he sat he could see the lake and the houseboat.

A few minutes after 17.30, he saw a motorboat coming across the lake.

*   *   *

Toni had been hitting the bottle and now he was full of whisky courage and lust. He had borrowed a coat from Salvadore so he could wear his gun harness and he had taken care to clean, oil and check the gun before leaving Little Creek.

He didn't expect trouble, but he was ready for it. His fear of Johnny was damped down by whisky and the thought of Freda.

As he reached the houseboat, he cut the engine and let the boat drift up as Freda came out on deck.

"Hi!" she said. "I was hoping you'd come." She caught the rope he tossed to her and made the boat fast. "I bet you could use a drink?"

"Yeah." Toni scrambled on deck. His hand went inside his coat and eased the gun for a quick draw. He looked around, very tense now.

"Well, come on in." Freda turned and walked into the living-room.

Moving like a cat, keeping close to her so if there was trouble her body would shield him, Toni moved into the room. One quick glance told him they were alone.

"Let's take a look around, baby," he said. "I like to know we're strictly on our own."

She laughed.

"You men! Johnny was the same. Scared my husband was hidden somewhere with a shotgun. Come on, then."

Leading the way, she took him from her bedroom to the other two bedrooms, into the kitchen, into the shower room. She even opened a big closet for him to inspect.

Then turning, a jeering look in her bright blue eyes, she said, "Satisfied?"

Toni grinned. He was now completely relaxed.

"Sure ... let's have that drink."

She led him back into the living-room.

"Sorry there's only coke. We can't afford liquor."

Toni blew out his cheeks, but maybe a coke was better. He knew he was already loaded.

"Fine." He sat down, eyeing her as she left him to go into the kitchen. She came back with a coke and handed it to him.

He leered at her, drank, then leered again.

"Some chick!"

"That's what Johnny was always saying."

"Your half-brother?"

She laughed and sat down away from him.

"I've never had a brother ... half or otherwise." She winked at him. "Strictly between ourselves, a girl has to be respectable in this dreary neck of the woods. Johnny was a stray my husband picked up, but he was good in bed."

Toni became alert.

"What's happened to him?"

She shrugged.

"Ships that pass in the night."

"What the hell does that mean?"

"He stayed three nights. He left early this morning. He was a nice guy ... but funny in a way." She looked at him. "He was superstitious. Are you superstitious?"

"Me? No."

"He was always talking about a St Christopher medal he had lost. It seemed to prey on his mind."

Johnny! Toni leaned forward.

"Where did you say he was going?"

"Miami. He had money. He said he was going to hire a boat and go to Havana. Now, why should anyone want to go there?"

"Did he have any baggage with him?"

"A big suitcase. It was heavy: even he had trouble with it." She cocked her head on one side. "Why the interest?"

177

Toni sat still, thinking. This was important information. He knew he should get back fast and telephone Luigi. They might pick up this sonofabitch in Miami before he hired a boat. Then he looked at Freda. Maybe an hour wouldn't make any difference.

He stood up.

"Let's you and me find out if one of those beds is soft," he said.

She laughed.

"That's what you're here for, isn't it?"

Breathing fast, his unsteady fingers unbuckling his gun harness, Toni followed her into her bedroom.

*   *   *

Sitting in the shade and cursing the mosquitoes that were buzzing around him, Johnny saw Toni come out on deck and get into the motorboat. He looked at his strap watch. Toni had been in there for an hour. Johnny didn't need to exercise his imagination to know what those two had been doing. He felt a cold bitterness towards her. How could she tell him she loved him?

He waited until Toni's boat was out of sight, then he walked quickly across the jetty and into the living-room.

He heard her in the kitchen. He went to the door to find her making pastry. In a casserole, the pigeon breasts were simmering.

"It's all right," she said, seeing him in the doorway, and quickly she told him what she had said to Toni. "I sold it to him. I know he's convinced."

Johnny drew in a deep breath. If Toni now convinced Massino of this story, then the heat would be off. Massino would know that he (Johnny), once in Havana, would be out of his reach.

"I told him you had a heavy suitcase with you," Freda went on. She paused while she rolled out the pastry. "That was smart, wasn't it, Johnny?"

But in spite of what she had done for him, in spite of her cleverness, Johnny could only think of the hour she had spent with Toni alone.

"Did you enjoy his company?" he asked, his tone bitter.

She looked at him, her eyes suddenly stony.

"Is that all you have to say … no thanks?"

He moved uneasily.

"I'm asking you … did you enjoy his company? You got laid, didn't you?"

She began to line a pie-dish with the pastry. He stood there, waiting. He watched her tip the contents of the casserole into the pie-dish.

"Didn't you?"

"That's right."

He wanted to hit her but he controlled the urge.

"You're nothing but a whore, aren't you?"

She covered the pie-dish with pastry, then she put the dish into the oven.

"Aren't you?"

"Yes." She turned and faced him. "Before I married Ed I was a busy, busy call girl. He knew it and now you know it." Without looking at him again, she washed her hands under the tap, dried them, and moving past him, she went into the living-room. He hesitated, then followed her, feeling ashamed and defeated.

"I'm sorry," he said. "Thank you for what you've done for me. Forget what I said."

She sat down.

"That man meant no more to me than dozens of other men who have paid for it." She looked directly at him. "While he was getting rid of his dirty lust, I was thinking of you. You're the only one, Johnny, who has ever turned me on." She shrugged. "Can't you see, if you can get this stupid jealousy out of your mind, that I had to do it? I had to have him here to convince him you had gone and to convince him you're heading for Havana. If I had held back, he wouldn't have believed me. Can't you see that? Now, you're safe."

Johnny went to her and put his arms around her.

"I'm sorry baby. You mean so much to me. I'm sorry."

"Forget it." She kissed him, then she got to her feet and went to the window to stare across the lake. "So what are we going to do now? You mustn't show yourself. Can't we go tomorrow ... can't we get away?"

"Not yet. Although it's safer, baby, the way you've fixed it, it's also a lot more complicated."

"How do you mean?"

"If we took off tomorrow Ed would ask questions. He'd talk to Salvadore who would then know you lied to Toni. Then he'd start a hunt, not only for me, but for you. We have to wait at least another four days."

She lifted her hands in despair.

"Wait ... that's all I do ... wait!"

Then they heard the sound of the truck approaching and she went into the kitchen.

* * *

Massino was looking at the weekly Numbers figures that Andy had given him when Toni came on the line, calling from Little Creek.

Massino looked at Andy.

"It's Toni. Get on the extension and write down what he says!" Then to Toni, he barked, "Did you find him?"

"No, Mr Joe. I missed him by six hours. He was here, but he's gone now. The chick says he's headed for Miami to hire a boat for Havana."

"Havana?" Massino's voice shot up.

"Yeah."

"Well, come on, come on! Give me the details!"

Toni told him all he knew. He was careful not to give details of his visit to Freda. He said she gave him a description of Johnny, mentioned the medal, said he had been holed up there for three nights and had gone off, carrying a heavy suitcase.

"So what do you want me to do, Mr Joe?"

Massino's mind raced.

"I'll call you back. Stick around," and taking Salvadore's number, he hung up.

"If he's got to Havana we're bitched!" he said, glaring at Andy. "And he's got the money!"

"So she says," Andy said quietly.

Massino stiffened.

"What's that supposed to mean?"

"I think we should check her story out, Mr Joe," Andy said. "You're right, if he's heading for Havana and Luigi doesn't pick him up before he leaves Miami then we kiss him and the money good-bye, but this could be a bluff. Toni's got nothing between his ears. He'd fall for any story a woman fed him. Let's check the woman first."

Massino thought about this, then nodded.

"I'll talk to Luigi. Got his number?"

"I'll get it." Andy went into his office and returned a few minutes later. "He's on the line now."

Massino snatched up the receiver.

"Luigi? How are you? Long time no see. What's that? Yeah ... sure is a big steal. Yeah. Listen. How about a little help? This woman ..."

He looked across at Andy who said, "Freda Scott, Little Creek."

"Yeah ... Freda Scott, lives at Little Creek. Salvadore knows all about her. She says Bianda took off early this morning, heading for Miami and then Havana. She could be lying. I want you to send someone out there and talk to her and when I say talk I mean give her the goddamn works. I want her squeezed dry! Don't let up until you're sure she's telling the truth ... get it? If you have to knock her off, knock her off. Will you do this for me, Luigi?"

"Sure, Joe." Luigi sounded expansive. "I've got a couple of bums who'd take real pleasure in a job like that, but it'll cost. How's about a grand: guaranteed results?"

"Come on, Luigi ... you're my friend. You wouldn't rob me, would you?"

"No more than you'd rob me, Joe. A grand and a guarantee."

"Suppose she's telling the truth?"

"Well, then you'll know, won't you?"

Massino cursed.

"Okay. Just get moving!" and he hung up.

At the other end of the line, Luigi knocked ash off his cigar and grinned to himself. He liked nothing better than easy money and this money couldn't be easier. The time was 21.15. No point in rushing this. Besides he had to supervise his restaurant. He called Salvadore and told him to send Toni back to the Waterfront Bar.

When Toni entered Luigi's office, he found two men propping up the wall while Luigi, at his desk, cigar gripped between his teeth, was checking the restaurant's booking.

The two men startled Toni. He was used to tough types but these two seemed to him to have escaped from a zoo. The bigger of the two had the broken face of a boxer, massively built and with a moronic grin, little beady eyes and no ears. They had probably been bitten off in some past brawl, Toni decided. The other was younger, thin, blond with expressionless eyes and a thin mouth and the deadpan expression of a pot smoker.

"Come on in," Luigi said. "The big one's Bernie. The other's Clive. They're going to talk to your chick. Mr Joe gets the idea she's lying so I'm sending the boys to shake the crap out of her." Luigi looked at Toni and grinned. "How was she as a lay?"

"Okay, Mr Luigi."

"Fine. You're lucky. She won't be much after these two have worked her over. Just wise up. When's the best time for a visit?"

"Her husband leaves at five-thirty in the morning. She's on her own then," Toni said uneasily.

Luigi looked at the two propping up the wall.

"Suppose you get over there around six? Don't worry about interrupting her coffee. Mr Joe's anxious for news, and don't worry about her. It's a big lake."

The two nodded and went away leaving Toni standing, uneasy and staring at Luigi. Even he, tough as he was, hated the thought of a chick like Freda in the hands of those two apes.

"Okay, Toni," Luigi said, "go and enjoy yourself. Everything's on the house. If you want a girl tell the barman. He'll fix you. Have a ball."

Toni went to the bar and got drunk.

*   *   *

183

The sound of the truck starting up woke Johnny. He looked out of the window. There was mist on the lake and he could see the red rim of the sun coming up behind the pines. He looked at his watch. The time was 05.30. He reached for a cigarette and listened to the truck backing out of the parking bay, then go roaring up the dirt road.

The evening had passed with the help of the television. Freda's pigeon pie had been a success. Scott had congratulated him on his shooting. Johnny had slept badly, continually waking, dozing, then waking again. Now, a cigarette between his lips, he took stock of his position.

If Massino was convinced by Freda's story, the heat must cool. But would he be convinced? He (Johnny) would have to stay under cover for at least another four days, then he would have to get to a telephone and call Sammy. He wouldn't dare show himself in Little Creek. Where else was a telephone? He would have to ask Freda that. If Sammy could assure him the heat was off, then he and Freda would go back to East City, take a chance, collect the money and get out of town. If Massino was sure he was in Havana, he could see no danger in again driving south. Problems! First getting to a telephone and then getting a car. There was no question now of Freda hiring a car from Little Creek. Maybe they would have to walk to New Symara ... some walk in this heat!

He threw off the sheet and got out of bed. A cup of coffee would go well with his cigarette.

"Johnny?"

Freda came out of her bedroom. Her blonde hair was mussed, but to Johnny, with the softness of sleep still on her, she looked beautiful.

"Just getting coffee, baby. Want some?"

"Hmmm."

She went into the bathroom.

As Johnny poured coffee into a saucepan, he thought about her. A whore! So what? Lots of women were whores, trading their bodies not for money but for presents, jewels, furs ... whatever they yearned for. She was his woman, he told himself. Who cares about anyone's past if there is love and Johnny knew he was in love with her. He wasn't much anyway, but he would be! $186,000 made any man something!

He could feel it was going to be hot and he thought with dismay that from now on there would be no swimming, no fishing. He would have to stay out of sight.

He poured the hot coffee into a cup and as he was about to pour more coffee into a second cup, he heard a car drive up.

Moving swiftly, he put the second cup away, then darted into his bedroom, snatched up his gun, pulled the sheet up over the bed, then darted into Scott's bedroom, the window of which gave a view onto the jetty.

He saw a dusty Lincoln parked at the foot of the jetty and from it spilled two men: one big, like an ape, the other small, white-faced with staring eyes. They both wore black suits, white shirts and white ties. They stood looking around, then they started across the jetty, taking their time as Johnny moved into the passage.

Freda, still in her shortie nightdress, was standing in the bathroom door.

"Trouble," Johnny said softly. "Don't worry. I'll take care of it."

"No! Get out of sight!" Freda whispered fiercely. "I'll take care of it! Get in the closet and wait!"

She caught hold of his arm and shoved him towards the big closet. For a moment he hesitated, then when a knock sounded on the door, he slid into the closet and shut the door.

Freda ran into her bedroom, snatched up a wrap and struggled into it as the knock came again.

She braced herself, then went to the door and opened it. When she saw Bernie and Clive, she felt a rush of cold blood up her spine. But she kept control of herself.

"What do you want?"

Bernie, smelling of sweat, his moronic grin terrifying, moved forward, forcing her back.

"You, dolly-bird. We want to talk to you about Johnny." But it was the other one Freda feared: the little, white-faced horror with his evil, sadistic eyes who followed behind the ape man.

"He's gone," she said.

They were now in the living-room and she had retreated to the far wall.

"Tell us about him, dolly-bird. We're looking for him," Bernie said.

"He left yesterday."

"That's what we heard." Bernie shuffled forward and snatched off her wrap leaving her in her shortie nightdress. "Yeah, we heard that," then he slapped her across her face so violently she bounced back against the wall and then sprawled on the floor. He reached down and tore off her nightdress, "but we don't believe it, dolly-bird. Feed us another story."

She lay naked at his feet, staring up at him.

"He went to Miami yesterday morning early," she said, her voice steady. "Get out of here, you apes!"

Bernie sniggered.

"Go ahead, Clive, work on her," he said. "When you're tired, I'll take over."

In the closet, Johnny listened. He quietly opened the closet door, gun in hand and moved into the passage. He was wearing only pyjama trousers, his feet were bare and he made no sound as he entered the living-room.

Clive had caught hold of Freda and had hauled her to her feet. He was setting himself to slap her as Johnny killed him.

The bang of the gun made Freda scream. She hid her face in her hands and dropped to her knees.

Clive, shot through the back of his head, heaved forward and fell.

Snarling, Bernie, groping for his gun, spun around to face Johnny who shot him through the face. The big man crashed down on top of Clive, his right arm catching Freda on the back of her neck as he fell. She sprawled on her face, then twisted and half sat up, staring at the two dead men, her eyes wide with horror, her mouth open in a soundless scream.

Dropping his gun, Johnny went to her, got her to her feet and half carried, half dragged her into her bedroom. He laid her gently on the bed.

"Stay here. Don't think about a thing."

He ran into his room and struggled into his shirt and trousers. He slid his feet into his shoes, then he returned to the living-room.

Freda lay still, her eyes closed. She struggled with hard, dry, choking sobs. It seemed to her she lay there for a long time. She couldn't move. The horror of seeing the two men shot dead paralysed her.

The sun was climbing and it came through the open window, hurting her eyes. She put her arm across her face, moaning.

She lay there, not caring, wanting only to believe this was a horrible nightmare.

Then a hand touched her gently.

"Let's go, baby," Johnny said. "Come on. This is where we duck out."

She opened her eyes and stared up at him.

"Go ... where?"

"We have their car. It's our chance. We've got to go!"

He hauled her off the bed and she leaned against him.

"What's happened ... those men?"

"Forget them. They're in the lake. Get dressed. We've got to hurry ... every minute is important."

She stood in a daze, staring at him.

"Come on, baby!" His voice sharpened. "Get dressed! You've got to pack! Hurry!"

"You killed them! I can't go with you! You killed them!"

"You can't not go with me," Johnny said. "Get dressed!"

Those words made an impact. She shuddered, then making an effort, she opened her closet and took from it the man's shirt and the stretch pants. Her closet was pathetically bare: a cheap cotton dress, a pair of worn Levis, a pair of broken down shoes.

She pulled on her panties and the stretch pants.

"You want to take any of this other junk?"

"No."

"Come on." He waited until she had put on the shirt and run a comb through her hair, then he led her into the living-room. "You've got to write a letter to Ed. Got any writing paper?"

Shaking, she sat at the table.

"In that drawer."

He found a block of cheap notepaper and an envelope. He found a biro.

"Write this: Dear Ed. I'm sick of it here. I'm going with Johnny. We love each other, Freda."

Somehow she wrote the note, her hand shaking. Johnny put it in the envelope and laid it on the table.

"Let's go!"

He picked up his suitcase and, taking her by her arm, he hurried her across the jetty to the Lincoln.

As he started the motor, he looked at his strap watch. The time was 06.40. At best, he thought, they had a three hour start before Luigi would begin to wonder where the two apes had got to. Then he would investigate, phone, and the organization would swing into action.

In a car like this you could go some way in three hours.

Driving steadily, with Freda still in shock at his side, he headed for the freeway.

189

10

They had been driving for over an hour in silence. Johnny kept the car moving but he was careful to keep just under the speed limit. He knew it would be a disaster for both of them if they were stopped by a speed cop. He longed to let the powerful car out and put more mileage behind him, but he restrained himself.

He by-passed Daytona Beach, anxious not to get snarled up in any heavy traffic, and kept on up Highway 1, heading north. As he drove, his mind was active. From time to time, he glanced at Freda who was staring through the windshield, her face white, her eyes blank. He could see the shock was still hitting her. Well, now they were out in the open, he thought and in a stolen car. He was safe enough for another two hours, then he would have to get rid of the car.

All kinds of problems crowded in on him, but he refused to be panicked. They now knew he was wearing a beard so that had to come off. They knew he wore khaki drill. He would have to change his clothes. Salvadore would give them a description of Freda. He looked at her blonde, silky hair. That was like a beacon to anyone hunting for them. That would have to be fixed.

Suddenly she said, "Where are we going?"

He drew in a deep breath of relief.

"How are you feeling, baby?"

"I'm all right." Her voice was shaky. "Where are we going?"

"We're driving north. We have another two hours before they start wondering. In two hours we'll be at St David's Bay. We'll stop there. It's a vacation town: packed with tourists and cars. We'll have to get rid of this car. Don't worry. Take it easy. Leave it to me."

"Oh, Johnny, I'm frightened!" She put her hand on his thigh. "Did you have to kill them?"

"I warned you, baby, this is the Mafia. You kill or get killed," Johnny said quietly. "I still think we have a chance. I'll tell you now: there's $186,000 in those bags. I'm telling you because you are now in this mess as much as I am. I'm sorry, but you are and you've got to realize it. There's still a good chance we can get the money and get away with it."

"A hundred and eighty-six thousand!" Her voice shot up. "But, Johnny, that's a fortune!"

"That's it. Well, you know now. It's a gamble: our lives against that money. If I get it, we'll share it. I mean that."

"So what do we do?"

"When we get to St David's Bay, go to a hairdresser and get them to tint your hair any colour you like, but the word will have gone out to look for a blonde. I'll get this beard off. We've got to buy clothes. I've got the money. You don't have to worry about that. Then we've got to ditch this car. We'll take a Greyhound bus to Brunswick. There we'll hole up and wait. We have enough money. We can wait two months if we have to. Then when my contact in East City tells me the heat is off, we go collect the money."

"Do you think we'll get it?"

"If we don't, we're dead," he said, knowing this was the truth.

It was 09.50 when they drove into St David's Bay. Johnny saw a vast free car park by the beach crammed with cars and caravans.

"This is where we ditch the car." He drove into the car park. It took him several minutes to find a space, but he found one. "From now on we walk."

He unlocked his suitcase and took out what was left of Sammy's money.

"This is how much we have got," he said and counted the money while she watched him. "Two thousand, eight hundred and fifty-seven dollars. I want you to see this, baby. I want you to know that from now on we are together, partners." He counted out a thousand and handed her the bills. "You have this, just in case something happens to me. Go find a hairdresser and get your hair fixed, then buy clothes. Don't spend much. We could have to live on this for some time. Be careful what you buy: nothing that'll catch the eye. We'll be husband and wife. I've been thinking. We two are on vacation, travelling Greyhound and seeing the country. I'm giving you the background. We take a room in some little hotel in Brunswick. You tell them I've a bad heart and I have to take it easy. We won't go out much. You think it was a mistake for us to come so far. I'm in need of a rest. We sign in as Mr and Mrs Henry Jackson from Pittsburgh. This is only rough thinking. We'll polish it later."

She put the money he had given her in her bag, then she looked at him.

"While I'm getting my hair fixed, Johnny, do you plan to leave me?"

This shocked him. For a long moment, he stared at her, then smiled.

"Ask yourself. It's only in oneself that one knows trust, baby."

Closing the suitcase, he got out of the car.

She joined him.

"I'm sorry." She touched his arm. "I've known so many men. I'm so sick of myself! I don't know who to trust."

"If you can't trust me by now, baby," he said gently, "then you're in real trouble. Come on, let's go."

They walked into the town. Although it was early, the tourists were out in force, heading for the beach. Half-way down the Main street, Johnny spotted the Greyhound bus station.

"We meet there." He pointed. "Be as quick as you can. I'll wait for you ... you wait for me. Okay?"

She hated him leaving her.

"Johnny ... I'm scared to be on my own ... really scared."

He smiled at her.

"But, baby, we're always alone. I've been alone all my life and so have you. Just get your hair fixed and buy some clothes. You'd better buy a hold-all." He looked around. "Up there on the left: a Ladies' hairdressers. Get your hair fixed first."

"Yes." She forced a smile. "See you, Johnny."

"That's one thing you can be sure of."

They parted and Johnny went in search of a barber.

*   *   *

Luigi was occupied with his Maitre d'hotel, arranging the menu for the following day when his telephone bell rang. The time was 11.05. He reached for the receiver as he said,

"Give 'em duck. We've got too many ducks in the freezer."
Then into the mouthpiece, he said, "Who is it?"

"This is Joe!" Massino's voice was tight with rage.
"What's happening? I've been waiting! What did that
whore say?"

Luigi stiffened. He had been so occupied with the routine
work of his restaurant, he had completely forgotten he had
sent Bernie and Clive out to Little Creek.

"Still waiting, Joe. I should hear any minute. The
moment I hear I'll call you back."

"What the hell are those punks doing?" Massino bawled.
"Get me some action!" and he hung up.

Luigi was now worried. He had told those two to see the
girl at 06.00. Five hours ago! He snatched up the receiver.
"Get Capello here!" he barked, cut the connection, then
dialled Salvadore's number. "What's going on?" he
demanded. "Bernie and Clive were supposed to see this
whore at six this morning. What's happening?"

"I don't know." Salvadore said. "I haven't seen them.
Hold for a moment." After a minute or so, he came back on
the line. "Just looked at the houseboat through my glasses.
No sign of life."

"I'm sending Capello. Go with him and find out what's
happening." Luigi's voice was now a snarl. "Call me back
pronto."

An hour later, as Little Creek's church clock was striking
twelve, Toni arrived at the store in a car Luigi had lent him.
Salvadore was waiting for him.

"What gives?" Salvadore asked.

"I don't know. We've got to get over there and find out."

They climbed into Salvadore's boat and headed across
the lake to the houseboat. Toni was first on deck, gun in
hand. He was sweating and he had a hell of a headache

from his heavy drinking the previous evening. Salvadore tied up and joined him. They went through the deserted houseboat, then Toni saw an envelope lying on the table. He opened it and read the message.

"Hey! Look at this! That bastard was here all the time! They've gone off together!"

"But where's Bernie and Clive?" Salvadore looked around, then knelt, putting his hand on the worn carpet. "Been recently washed." The two men looked at each other, then Salvadore went out on deck, staring into the clear water on the lake. Toni joined him.

"You think he knocked them off?"

"How the hell do I know?" Salvadore went back into the living-room and shoved the table aside. He found a small patch of dried blood that Johnny had missed in spite of his careful cleaning up. "Look."

Toni peered over his shoulder.

"So he did knock them off," he said huskily.

"Yeah and he's taken their car. You'd better talk to Mr Luigi and fast."

Twenty-five minutes later, Toni was reporting to Luigi. Five minutes later, Luigi was reporting to Massino.

Massino was so incensed he could hardly speak. Finally, he screamed, "You get nothing from me! I'll talk to the Big Man! You're as useless as a broken leg!"

"Take it easy, Joe. I've alerted the cops to find the car," Luigi said, sweating. "I've lost two good men. You can't talk this way to me."

"No? You'll see! I'll give you thirty-six hours to find them or I talk to the Big Man!" and Massino slammed down the receiver.

Luigi thought for a long moment, then he put a call through to his Don who ruled Florida. He explained the situation, and gave a detailed description of Johnny and Freda.

"Okay," the Don said. "As soon as the cops have located the car, let me know. We'll find them."

"Massino says he gives me thirty-six hours. He's raging mad," Luigi said uneasily.

The Don laughed. "Forget it. Massino's just a bag of wind. I'll talk to the Big Man myself," and he hung up.

*   *   *

Freda stood outside the Greyhound bus station, clutching a small holdall. She had been waiting for twenty minutes. She looked constantly from left to right, but she could see no sign of Johnny. Her heart was beating violently and she felt sick with fear.

"You sucker!" she told herself. "Of course he's walked out on you! What did you expect? All that money! Why should he share it? $186,000! To think so much money exists! Men! God! How I hate them! They've only one thought in their filthy minds!"

"Sorry to keep you waiting, baby. I scarcely recognize you. You look great."

She spun around, staring at the short, thick-set man at her side, her heart leaping. For a moment she didn't know him. He was clean shaven except for his heavy moustache and he had had his head shaved, Yul Brynner style. He was wearing grey flannel slacks, a white shirt and a lightweight dark-blue jacket.

"Oh, Johnny!"

She made a move towards him, her voice breaking, but he drew back.

"Watch it!" The snap in his voice stiffened her. "Later. I've got the tickets. It held me up. Come on, let's go."

She was so relieved he hadn't deserted her, she wanted to cry, but she controlled herself. She followed him to the bus and they climbed in.

Johnny regarded her as they sat at the back of the bus, nodding his approval. She too had changed her appearance. She was now a redhead and it suited her. She was wearing a dark-green trouser suit and big sun goggles. He eyed every passenger who boarded the bus, but he saw no one to alert an alarm.

It wasn't until the bus began to roar along the freeway that he put his hand on hers.

"You look really great, baby," he said, "but I still like you better blonde. You got everything you want?"

"Yes. I spent over a hundred dollars, Johnny."

"Okay, okay," he said and again pressed her hand.

"Oh, Johnny, I was scared ... I began to wonder ..."

"We're both scared, but it could work out. It's worth a try, isn't it?"

She thought of all that money: $186,000!

"Yes."

They sat in silence for some minutes, then Johnny said, "Look, baby, I want you to know your position. I know this is a bit late in the day, but I have it on my mind. There's still time for you to opt out ... at least I think so. Maybe we've left it too late, but maybe, you still have a chance of opting out."

She stared at him, her eyes widening.

"I don't know what you're saying."

"I keep thinking about it," Johnny said. "I keep asking myself if I should drag you into this. Sooner or later they will catch up with me. When the Mafia sign goes up, you're as good as dead. I mean this, but with luck, if I get the money, if I can buy my boat I'll settle for twelve months. I could be more than lucky and it might be three years ... but no more. Who goes with me also gets the sign. They may not bother with you right now, but if they find out we are together when they catch up with me ... and they will eventually ... then it'll be the end of your days as it will be the end of mine."

She shivered.

"I don't want to hear this, Johnny. Please ..."

"You've got to hear it. There's a chance. We could survive three years. We'd be beating the odds if we survive longer, but sooner or later, they'll get me and, baby, please think about what I'm saying. Don't imagine if they get me they'll forget you. They don't work like that. They'll come after you. You could hide, but sooner or later there'll come a knock on your door and it'll be them. I want you with me, but I want you to realize the risk. Think about it. We stand a chance, but not for long. If I get the money, I'll fix it you get a big cut. This I promise you so you don't have to worry about losing out. In half an hour we'll get to Jacksonville. You could get off there and get lost. They could forget about you while hunting for me. You have some money now. You know how to take care of yourself. I hate to say it, but I feel it in my bones for your safety you should get off at Jacksonville."

She closed her eyes, feeling the jogging motion of the bus and she tried to think, but nothing came into her mind except that immense sum of money: $186,000!

Three years of life?

With all that money she could have a ball of a time!

So suppose they caught up with them as Johnny seemed to think they would? So suppose they walked in and shot them to death as Johnny had shot those two apes to death?

What was death anyway? She tried to believe it as an escape.

But three years with $186,000 ... that would be living!

She sat there, her eyes closed and reviewed her own life. What a stinking, hell of a life! Her dreary home, her dreary parents, the gruesome men in and out of her life, Ed and the boredom!

But at the back of her mind was the fear of the moment when a knock could come on the door. She forced the fear away and opened her eyes. Somehow she managed to smile.

"You and me, Johnny, together. I don't opt out."

The bus roared north and they sat, hand in hand, silent now, but both knowing whatever the future, they could now trust each other.

* * *

Sammy the Black rolled out of bed around 07.30. Feeling depressed and half asleep, he went into the shower room. Fifteen minutes later he emerged, shaved and showered and started the coffee percolator.

He had a number of reasons for feeling depressed, but the main reason which had kept him awake half the night was that Cloe had got herself pregnant again. How the hell this could have happened defeated Sammy. She swore she was on the pill, and now she was yelling for a quick abortion ... and that cost! They had had a distressing meeting last night. She demanded $300!

"I'm not having any of your bastards!" she had shrilled. "Come on ... give me the money!"

But he had no money. Johnny had taken all his savings. He didn't tell her this, but he did say he had no $300.

She had stared at him, her big, black eyes glittering.

"Okay, if you haven't the bread, I'll look elsewhere. Jacko wants me and he'll pay."

Sammy had regarded her: lush, tall, with a body like a goddess, and his heart quailed. He couldn't lose her! He knew Jacko: a big, black buck who was always on the fringe of her life, waiting.

"Give me a little time, honey," he pleaded. "I'll get the money somehow."

"I'll give you six days ... no more!"

That was one problem: then his goddamn brother was again in trouble. Sammy's mother had come to him. Only a matter of $300. "You can't let your brother go to jail!"

Sammy had promised to do something ... but what?

Then his job as Mr Joe's chauffeur. Driving a Rolls had sounded fine. The grey uniform with its black piping had made Sammy proud and happy, but he quickly learned this was a job without a song. He was on constant call. After he had driven Mr Joe to his office, he had to rush back up town to take Mrs Joe shopping and, man! was she a bitch! She always seemed to want to go to some shop where parking was impossible and he had to circle and circle, getting snarled up in the traffic, and if he kept her waiting did she curse him and could she curse! Sammy thought wistfully of those days when he had collected the Numbers money with Johnny. He had been scared, but being scared was better than this rat race. Then in the evening Mr and Mrs Joe went to nightclubs and he had to sit in the car until after 02.00 waiting for them. He had to keep the car immaculate or Mrs Joe would curse him. What a mug he had been to take this job!

Wearily, he got into his uniform. He had to pick up Mr Joe at nine. It took him a good half hour to drive up town against the traffic. As he was sipping his coffee, his telephone bell rang. He winced. This could be Cloe, screaming at him again. He hesitated, then lifted the receiver as if it were a ticking bomb.

"Sammy?"

A rush of cold blood went down his spine and he began to shake. This was too much!

Johnny!

"Yeah ... this is me," Sammy said huskily.

"Listen, Sammy, I want you to go to the Greyhound bus station and take a look around. I want to know if it's still staked out."

"Mr Johnny ... I can't! I've got enough troubles. You took my money. Cloe is in trouble again. My brother is in trouble again. Everyone is yelling me!" Sammy was close to tears. "Please leave me alone."

"This is important, Sammy!" Johnny's voice was hard. "You've got to do it! You do it and I promise you I'll give you back your money plus another three thousand dollars. I promise you!"

Sammy stiffened.

"You really mean that, Mr Johnny?"

"Have I ever let you down? You check the bus station and if it's clear, you'll get six thousand ... that's a promise."

Sammy hesitated.

"But suppose it ain't clear?"

"Then you keep checking and as soon as it's clear, you'll get the money."

Again Sammy hesitated. Six thousand dollars! Cloe would get her abortion! His goddamn brother would be in the clear and he'd have money back in his steel box!

"Okay, Mr Johnny, I'll do it."

"I'll call you this time tomorrow," and Johnny hung up.

Sammy was shaking with fear, but if he could get hold of six thousand dollars all his troubles would be over! And when Mr Johnny made a promise, it was a promise.

Putting on his peak cap, he left his apartment and walked fast to the garage. Why was Mr Johnny so anxious to know if the bus station was being watched? Sammy cringed. It could mean only one thing, but he refused to let his mind dwell on it.

He drove Massino to his office.

"Get home pronto," Massino said. "Mrs Massino has shopping to do. We'll be going out tonight. She'll tell you about it." He paused to look at Sammy, seeing his grey complexion and the sweat glistening on his face. "What's the matter with you?"

"Nothing, boss," Sammy said, cringing. "I'm fine, boss." Massino grunted, then strode across the sidewalk into his office building.

Sammy looked across at the Greyhound station, then after a long hesitation, he got out of the Rolls.

As Massino entered his office, he found Andy standing at the window.

"Let's get at it," Massino barked. "Have you got ..." He stopped as Andy raised his hand, then beckoned to him. Frowning, Massino joined him at the window. He saw Sammy crossing the street, look furtively right and left, hesitate, then enter the bus station.

"What's that big bastard doing?" Massino growled. "I told him to get back right away to my wife."

"Watch it," Andy said quietly.

There was a long delay, then Sammy came out of the bus station, again looked furtively to right and left, then he crossed the street, got in the Rolls and drove away.

"So what?" Massino demanded.

He could see by Andy's expression that he had just seen something he didn't understand but Andy did.

"He looked like a dip, didn't he?" Andy said. "He was scared."

"That's right. I asked him what was the matter. He was sweating like a pig ... so what?"

Andy sat down by Massino's desk.

"All along I've thought Bianda wasn't working alone. I was sure someone helped him steal the money. I thought it was Fuselli. I never thought of Sammy."

Massino grew still, his eyes glittering.

"Bianda has worked with Sammy for years," Andy went on. "When you start to think about it, it sticks out like a boil. It's my bet Sammy is in contact with Bianda. The money's over there, Mr Joe, in one of those lockers and Sammy is checking to see if we're still covering the lockers. That's my reading. Bianda had to have someone to work with ... it's my bet Sammy rushed the two bags over to the locker while Bianda rushed back to establish his alibi."

Massino sat down, his face congested with rage.

"Get Ernie and Toni to pick up that sonofabitch and bring him here. I'll talk to him! I'll smash him to pulp!"

"No," Andy said quietly. "We want Bianda and the money. So we set a trap. This afternoon, you and me will take a drive uptown and with Sammy listening you'll tell me you've heard from Luigi that Bianda is now in Havana and you've kissed the money good-bye. We then call off the boys watching the lockers so when Sammy checks again he finds the coast clear. He'll tell Bianda and he'll come back."

Andy stared at Massino. "All we need is Toni sitting up here with a target rifle and a silencer."

"I want that bastard alive."

"It's better to have him dead and the money back, isn't it?"

Massino thought about this.

"Maybe."

"More than maybe, Mr Joe. We don't have to pay the Big Man. We handle this ourselves. It'll save us a lot of money." Massino showed his teeth in a savage grin.

"Now you're using your head." He patted Andy's arm. "At least I can take care of that big bastard." He brooded for a moment, his face savage. "And the whore."

11

The Greyhound bus had dropped them at the Brunswick bus station. Johnny had gone to the information desk and asked the girl for a decent, cheap hotel.

She was a pretty little thing with blonde curls and long, false eyelashes and she was helpful.

"You could call me biased," she said, "but my uncle runs the Welcome hotel. It's thirty dollars a day, everything included and the food's wonderful. That's for the two of you." She fluttered her eyelashes first at Freda, then at him. "Honest, you'll be happy there."

"Okay and thanks," Johnny said. "Where do I find it?"

"Third on the left up Main Street: it's not far."

Carrying their bags and with Freda at his side, Johnny walked up Main Street. He was a little worried about the price. He had no idea how long they would have to stay at the hotel.

But when they were shown into the big room, with a double bed, two comfortable arm chairs, a shower room and a colour TV set, Johnny ceased to worry.

They both took showers, then got on the bed.

They had spent the rest of the afternoon in each other's arms. Around 19.30, they went down to the restaurant and enjoyed a good meal.

Johnny was pleased to see Freda was much more relaxed and even gay. They watched TV until midnight, then went to bed. Neither of them spoke of the Mafia nor of the money, consciously enjoying this comfort, and desperately clinging to what they both knew was an interval free of danger.

The following morning, Johnny called Sammy. Freda, sitting up in bed, listened. When he hung up, they looked at each other.

"We'll know this time tomorrow," Johnny said.

"Do you think it'll be all right?"

"Your guess is as good as mine." He got back on the bed. "Baby, I want my boat. Do you mind?"

"Of course not. I want it too." She put her hand on his. "I want it for you because I love you."

Later, as he was dozing off, she said, "They'll never find us, will they?"

What was the use, after warning her, in telling her they could never escape? What was the use of telling her they were buying time? But he couldn't lie to her. In silence, he turned his hand to grip hers.

He felt her shiver and he knew she had got the message.

"Love me," she said, pulling him on to her. "Make me forget."

The day drifted by. They went down to the restaurant for lunch. They returned to their room and watched a ball game on TV. They went down to the restaurant for dinner, then returned to their room. They watched TV until after midnight.

Johnny didn't sleep much. He kept thinking of Massino. He was aware that Freda was having nightmares. Twice, she cried out, but by putting his hand on hers, he stilled her cries.

Soon after 07.30, he called Sammy.

"What's happening?"

"I got news," Sammy said, his voice excited. "Mr Joe is sure you're in Havana. He said he's kissed you goodbye."

Johnny's heart gave a little jump.

"How do you know that?"

"I had to drive Mr Joe and Mr Andy up town. Mr Joe was in a terrible mood: cursing and swearing. He told Mr Andy this Mr Luigi had telephoned. This gentleman said you were now in Havana and there was nothing more he could do. He said the money was gone." A pause, then Sammy asked, "You're not in Havana, are you, Mr Johnny?"

"Never mind where I am. Look, Sammy, check the bus station. I must know if the boys are still there. Will you do that?"

"Yeah, I'll do it."

"I'll call you back. When can I get you?"

"It's my night off. I'll be right here at five."

"I'll call you just after five."

"And, Mr Johnny, you still mean it about the six thousand bucks? I'm worrying about it: Cloe's giving me no peace."

"You'll get it. I told you: it's a promise."

When he had hung up, he told Freda what Sammy had said. They looked at each other.

"You know something, baby?" Johnny said, smiling at her. "I think you've saved us. It was your brainwave to have told them I was heading for Havana. I'd never have thought of it. This could be our break. If the locker isn't guarded and I'll know this evening, then we can get the money."

"Oh, God, Johnny! I prayed last night! I haven't prayed for years. So what do we do?"

"If we get the green light this evening, we hire a car and drive back to East City. We can do it in three hours. We'll arrive at the bus station around eleven o'clock. That's a good time. Not many people around and it will be dark. We get the money and we get out."

"I can't believe it!"

"It depends if the bus station is being watched. If it isn't, then we go."

"And Johnny, if they think we're in Havana ..." She paused to look at him. "Then no one will come knocking on our door."

"That's it, baby." He pulled her close to him. "No one will come knocking on our door."

* * *

As Sammy came out of the elevator, heading for Massino's office, Andy appeared. He stared at Sammy's grey, sweating face.

"Where do you think you're going?"

Sammy ducked his head in a servile bow.

"Just going to ask the boss if there was anything else for me to do. It's my night off, but I just wanted to ask him."

Andy was sure Massino wouldn't be able to control himself if he saw Sammy. Andy had tapped Sammy's telephone and the conversation between Sammy and Johnny was on tape and Massino had listened to it.

"It's okay," he said. "You push off. Mr Joe's busy right now."

Sammy nodded and got back into the elevator. Andy crossed to Massino's office, entered and closed the door.

Massino was at his desk. Leaning against the walls were Toni, Ernie, Lu Beriffi and Benno. On Massino's desk lay a .22 target rifle equipped with powerful telescopic sight and a silencer.

"Sammy's going home," Andy said and went to the window. "Toni, get the rifle and come here."

Puzzled, Toni looked at Massino who nodded. Toni picked up the rifle and followed Andy to the open window. Andy pulled up a straight-backed chair.

"Sit down. Look across the street. Look at the entrance to the bus station."

Toni did as he was told.

"Now look through the telescopic sight," Andy went on. "Focus on anyone."

Looking through the powerful sight, Toni was startled. A taxi driver, lolling against his cab and enjoying the sunshine came into focus and Toni felt he could reach out and touch his head.

"Man!" he muttered. "Some sight!"

"Keep watching. You'll see Sammy in a moment. I want you to get him in focus."

Massino shoved back his chair and joined them at the window. They watched Sammy cross the street and pause to look around. His movements were furtive.

"Got him?"

"Sure. I can see the sweat on his mug," Toni said. They watched Sammy edge into the bus station and disappear. They waited. After a few minutes, Sammy came out, again looked furtively around and then walked away.

"Could you have killed him?" Andy asked as Toni lowered the rifle.

"With this beauty? Sure! A kid of six could have knocked him off."

Andy looked at Massino.

"Maybe I'd better handle this, Mr Joe. Maybe it would be better if you were out of town."

Massino thought, then nodded.

"Yeah."

Looking at the other men, Andy said, "So let's get this operation set up. Sooner or later, Bianda will show." He turned to Toni. "You and me are going to sit at this window until he shows. When he does, you blow his head off."

Toni drew in a sigh of relief. He had been scared he might have to face Johnny in a gun fight, but now he knew he had only to sit at the window with a target rifle, he felt he could afford a grin.

"That'll be a pleasure," he said.

"You others stay out of sight downstairs. When Toni hits this bastard, you chase across the street, grab the two bags and come back here. It's got to be done fast. I've fixed it the cops will be out of the way, but not for long, so work fast." He turned to Massino, "You like it, Mr Joe?"

"Yeah. You're using your head. So okay, I'll take a week off in Miami." He stared at Andy. "When I get back, I expect the money in the safe and those three straightened out."

"That's my planning, Mr Joe."

"When you have the money, I want Sammy taken care of," Massino said to Benno. "Take Ernie with you and smear that sonofabitch across a wall. I mean that. Smash him to bits! Take a can of gas with you. When you've finished smearing him, set him on fire."

Benno grinned.

"Okay, boss."

Massino turned to Toni.

"There's the whore. You're the only one who's seen her. Take care of her. She'll run, but keep after her. Make her suffer. You don't work for me until you've found and fixed her, but you'll get paid."

Toni nodded.

"That'll be another pleasure."

When Massino had left the office, Andy said, "Okay, we can relax. Sammy gets a call from Bianda in another hour. In an hour's time, Bianda could try for the money. We have to get this organized. Bianda may be cagey. He might wait a week ... so, okay, we wait a week, but any minute of that week, he could show ... so we wait."

Waiting meant nothing to these men. They spent a third of their lives waiting.

Andy tapped Toni on his shoulder.

"When he shows, you have to nail him. Fluff this one and you get the treatment."

Toni patted the target rifle. "A kid of six ..."

* * *

The big, airy room with its double bed, its two armchairs and its TV set seemed to have shrunk. The traffic sounds coming through the open window seemed to have increased. Tension hung in the room like a black canopy.

In bra and panties, Freda lay on the bed, her arm across her eyes. Johnny sat by the telephone, his eyes on his strap watch.

"Can't you call him now?" Freda asked, lifting her arm to look at Johnny. "For God's sake! We've been waiting hours!"

"I warned you, baby," Johnny said gently, "this is a waiting game." Sweat was trickling down his face. "It's only five to five."

"I'll go crazy if we have to wait much longer. All my goddamn life, I've had to wait for something!"

"Who hasn't?" Johnny wiped his face with his handkerchief. "Everyone is waiting for something. Take it easy, baby. Think of the boat, the sea, the sun and you and me. Think of that."

Her arm went back across her eyes.

"Sorry, Johnny. I'm on edge."

On edge? Johnny suppressed a sigh. He looked at her, lying there, so desirable and to him, beautiful. On edge? He felt now the chill of fear. In spite of his warnings, she didn't seem to realize what kind of jungle they were heading for.

They waited, listening to the traffic, hearing a police whistle and in the distance, an ambulance siren. The tension in the room built up. The minute hand of Johnny's watch crawled on. Could a minute last so long?

"Johnny!" Freda sat up. "Please call him now."

"Okay, baby."

He picked up the receiver and dialled Sammy's number. Listening to the burr-burr-burr on the line, he thought of the moment when he unlocked the locker and pulled the two heavy bags out and he closed his eyes. All that money!

Then Sammy's voice came on the line.

"Who's that?"

"Sammy? Johnny. You checked the bus station?"

"I checked it, Mr Johnny. There's no one there."

Johnny leaned forward, his heart beginning to thump.

"You're sure?"

"Yeah. I went all over it. The boys have gone."

"Where's Toni?" Johnny knew Capello was the danger man.

"I don't reckon he's back yet, Mr Johnny. The boss sent him to Florida. I haven't seen him."

"Okay," Johnny thought for a moment. The way south and out of town would take him past Sammy's place. "Around midnight, I'll look in with the money. Be there."

"Six thousand, Mr Johnny?"

212

"That's it. Be there," and Johnny hung up. He looked at Freda who had got off the bed and was watching him. "It's okay. They really think we're in Havana. We'll leave here at seven-thirty. Let's pack. I'll fix a Hertz car."

"You really mean it's safe ... you'll get the money?"

Johnny put his fingers into his shirt to feel his St Christopher medal: it was a reflex action, but when his fingers felt nothing but the sweat-coated hairs of his chest, he again heard his mother's words: *as long as you wear it nothing really bad can happen to you.*

"We're going to try, baby. Nothing in this life is safe, but we're going to try."

He picked up the phone book, found the number of Hertz-rent-a-car and called them. They said they would deliver a car to the hotel at 19.00.

Freda pulled on her green trouser suit and she was doing her hair as Johnny hung up.

"The car's fixed," he said, then going to his suitcase, he took out his gun and harness.

Watching him, her eyes opened wide.

"What are you doing?"

"Just being careful, baby." He smiled at her. "I don't think we'll need it, but one never knows."

"You're frightening me, Johnny."

"Go on packing. This isn't the time to be frightened ... this is the time to look ahead ... to the future. This time tomorrow, you and me will be worth one hundred and eighty-six thousand dollars!"

"Yes."

While she was carefully folding her new clothes into the suitcase, Johnny looked out of the window at the blue sky and the white clouds. His fingers went to his shirt, then dropped away.

He saw the little plop of water as the medal had hit the lake. He knew he could be walking into a trap. Sammy might be betraying him. He knew that, but what else was there to live for? If he didn't try to get the money, sooner or later, they would find him. So he had to try. He just might be lucky. He just might have the boat for a few months, but this he was sure of ... they would never take him alive. He looked over at Freda as she shut the lid of the suitcase. She and he, he decided, must share this destiny. They could have luck. Again he thought of the boat. He thought of the medal. That was superstition. There was still luck left.

In less than four hours, he would know if luck meant anything.

* * *

The hours crawled by. The lights over the bus station were on. The crowds were thinning out. The big clock above the bus station read 23.00.

"I've got to take a pee," Toni said. "My back teeth are floating."

"Hurry it up!" Andy snapped and eased his aching muscles.

Toni put down the target rifle and went fast to Massino's toilet.

As he laid down the rifle, Johnny drove into the parking lot of the bus station.

"Here we are baby," he said, his heart thumping. "You take over. Now listen, if anything bad happens, drive away fast. You understand? Don't wait ... just go." He took from his hip pocket the last of Sammy's money and dropped the bills in her lap. "It'll be all right, but I want to be sure. Go back to the Welcome hotel. You understand?"

214

Freda shivered.

"Yes ... It will be all right, Johnny?"

He put his hand on hers.

"Don't be scared. I'll get the money and come right back. You take off as soon as I'm in. Head up street. It's easy. At the traffic lights you turn left. Don't drive too fast."

"Oh, Johnny!"

He pulled her to him and kissed her.

"It's going to work out."

"I love you."

"Those are the best words. I love you too," then he walked into the bright lights and towards the luggage lockers.

Andy spotted him. He wasn't fooled by his shaven head. He recognized Johnny's walk, his square shoulders, his short, thick-set body.

"Toni!!"

Freda shifted across the seat and under the steering wheel. She stared through the dusty windshield, seeing Johnny disappear into the station. She sensed he and she were in danger. Her mind raced. Could she live on a boat? She hated the sea. Maybe once they had all this money, she could persuade him to give up this boat idea. Her dream was a luxury villa somewhere in the sun and to meet interesting people. With all that money, people would converge on them. There would be a swimming pool, a Cadillac and servants. Once a year they would go to Paris where she would buy clothes. That would be life! A boat! Who the hell but Johnny wanted a boat!

Her fingers gripped the steering wheel.

There was time ... first the money. If he really loved her, she could talk him out of this stupid idea of buying a boat.

Johnny reached the locker. He paused, looking right and left. The locker aisle was deserted. A voice boomed over the tannoy system: "Last bus for Miami. No. 15." He sank the key into the lock, opened the door and dragged out the two heavy bags.

As he dumped them on the floor, his mind moved triumphantly to his dream: a forty-five-footer with shining brass work and he at the helm, steering out to sea with the spray against his face and the sun beating down on him. And in this image which flooded his mind, Freda took no part. It was he and the forty-five-footer and the rise and fall of the deck.

He grabbed up the bags and started back across the station towards where he had parked the car. He was still moving fast, within a few yards of the car, seeing Freda at the wheel, when his life exploded into darkness.

Freda saw him coming and she caught her breath in a gasp of relief. Then she saw a tiny red spot appear in his shaven head, the bags drop from his hands and his short, thick-set body fold to the ground.

She sat there petrified, watching a thin stream of blood flowing from Johnny's head. She heard a woman screaming. Then she saw three men come fast out of the shadows, snatch up the bags and disappear.

She pushed the gear lever to "Drive" and moved the car out of the parking lot.

Dry retching sobs shook her as she drove out of town.

*   *   *

Sammy prowled around his tiny room. He kept looking at his cheap alarm clock on the bedside table. The time was 01.30. Mr Johnny had said he would bring six thousand dollars to him by midnight. Cloe had telephoned. She had said that she would give him until tomorrow morning and then she would ask Jacko to take care of her. Sammy said for her not to worry. He would have the money for her and she could fix an appointment with her doctor any time tomorrow.

Again he looked at the clock.

Mr Johnny had promised. What was happening?

Then he heard footsteps coming up the stairs and he relaxed, relieved and now happy. Here was Mr Johnny with the money! How could he have doubted him? When Mr Johnny made a promise ... it was a promise!

A knock came on the door.

Six thousand dollars! He would take Cloe south after her operation. She had always wanted to see Miami. His goddamn brother would now be out of trouble! His mother would be happy!

Sammy danced across the room to open the door.

*   *   *

The fat, elderly man smiled at her. He was well dressed with dyed black hair and shiny white false teeth.

"Piss off," Freda said. "Try someone else."

The fat man grimaced, then walked down the long street to where other girls were waiting.

Freda leaned against the wall, trying to rest her aching feet. It was now two months since Johnny had died. The money he had given her had run out. She knew she had been extravagant, but she had to have some decent clothes. Now she was back on the game but Brunswick wasn't profitable. It was a town full of kinky, elderly men and she had promised herself she would never pander to perverts.

But, she told herself, she would now have to save enough money to go either south where the men would appreciate her talents and looks or go north and get into the call girl racket again.

As she leaned against the wall she thought of Johnny: a sweet guy. She could have married him. He and his dream boat! Well, everyone had to have their dreams. All that money ... so near ... so far!

It began to rain. The street now was deserted. The other girls had called it a night. She opened her shabby purse and checked her money ... thirteen dollars.

Well, money was money. She snapped her purse shut and started down the long street towards the tiny room she now called her home.

Toni Capello, who had been watching her for the past half hour, moved after her. His hand slid into his coat pocket and his fingers closed around the bottle of acid.

It was while Freda was undressing that she heard a knock on her door.

Wearily, she pulled on a wrap.

"Who's there?" she called.

The knock sounded again.

Without thinking, she crossed the room and opened the door.

>>> If you've enjoyed this book and would like to discover more great vintage crime and thriller titles, as well as the most exciting crime and thriller authors writing today, visit: >>>

The Murder Room
Where Criminal Minds Meet

themurderroom.com

www.ingramcontent.com/pod-product-compliance
Ingram Content Group UK Ltd.
Pitfield, Milton Keynes, MK11 3LW, UK
UKHW022315280225
455674UK00004B/312